Amy Cross is the author of more than 200 horror, paranormal, fantasy and thriller novels.

OTHER TITLES
BY AMY CROSS INCLUDE

1775

THE HAUNTING OF HADLOW HOUSE BOOK THREE

AMY CROSS

CONTENTS

1775

PROLOGUE

IT WAS, AS MANY would later write, the shot heard around the world.

As gunfire rang out, two militiamen ducked down into a shallow trench and worked frantically to reload their arms. Both men were bloodied, and both had suffered small injuries, but they were determined to get back into the fray. Fighting had raged for hours now, with British forces having massed in an attempt to defeat the Patriot army. The fate of two nations lay in the balance as the conflict grew, although on that sunny but smoky day few could have predicted the full scope and horror of the oncoming American Revolutionary War.

"There are too many of them," James Pitcairn said, still working to reload his rifle. "We'll never repel them."

"We'll have them back to Boston by sundown," Robert Carter replied, before turning and craning his neck to look over the top of the trench. "When an army has right on its side, its numbers swell beyond anything that can be seen."

"But the British -"

"The British can be damned!" Carter snapped angrily. "If we don't stand and fight now, we never will! And if you insist on doubting our prospects, then you might as well turn around and fight for King George instead."

"I never said that," Pitcairn muttered, clearly annoyed by the slight. "I just think that we need to better prepare for this offensive."

"We have prepared long enough," Carter told him. "At some point, we have to strike."

"And do you think the British will just sit back and let that happen?" Pitcairn asked. "How many men do they have to throw at the battle? More than we do, I'd wager."

"This is our land," Carter said, "and we will defend it. Besides, the British might think that they're safe at home, but I'm sure there are those on their soil who are preparing to strike."

"What do you mean?"

"Only that the British had better watch their

backs," Carter replied, allowing himself a faint smile. "I cannot tell you everything that I've heard, only that complacency might be the greatest threat to British interests. And although this battle today might be the loudest and brightest, there are other battles – quieter battles, ones they are not expecting – that will swing the balance. Now, are you ready?"

"As I'll ever be."

"Then let's waste no time," Carter said firmly. "We must fight for our freedom!"

With that rallying cry, the two men climbed out of the trench and returned to the battle. Within minutes they were both dead, their bodies crushed into the mud, but the cause for which they fought refused to die; as the battle spread and the losses mounted on both sides, the tide of history was beginning to turn. And far away, many thousands of miles beyond that battlefield, one of Robert Carter's predictions was in the process of coming true in a small English village that was – at that moment – in the grip of the most terrible rainstorm.

CHAPTER ONE

April 1775...

RAIN CRASHED DOWN, THRASHING the land and sending great rivers running through the narrow streets of Cobblefield.

"Can't this wait until tomorrow?" Timothy Baker asked wearily, as he pushed another box onto the back of the carriage. "I'm soaked to my skin!"

"We've waited two days already," Matheson Crowther muttered. "If we wait for a break in this foul weather, we might never get away. Besides, you're not the only one who's soaked, so stop complaining and get on with the task at hand."

Stepping back, he looked at the boxes that they had already managed to load onto the carriage.

They'd made slow progress and there was much more work to be done, but the weather – if anything – was actually getting worse. All around the street, rain was battering the roofs of houses, while the spire of St. Leonard's Church could be seen rising up high into the gloom. Matheson reached up and wiped some matted hair from across his forehead, but deep down he knew he was only delaying the moment when he'd inevitably have to get back to work.

"Come on, then," he said to Timothy. "I'm not -"

Before he could get another word out, he spotted a figure emerging from one of the nearby streets. Seeing another poor soul out in the rain was strange enough, but something about this particular figure caused Matheson to furrow his brow. The man – and it seemed to be a man, although visibility in the storm was bad – appeared to be staggering along, as if he could barely stay on his feet; a moment later, as if to prove that point, he stumbled and almost fell, only staying upright thanks to a well-positioned wall upon which he was able to lean.

"Hello," Matheson said under his breath, "what have we got here then?"

"Do you think he's drunk?" Timothy asked,

having also spotted the man.

"That was my first thought," Matheson replied, "but I'm inclined to believe now that he's -"

Suddenly the man tripped, slamming down against the road. Sighing, Matheson hurried past the carriage and made his way over, with Timothy just a few steps behind. As they both reached the man, they saw that he was trying but failing to get to his feet, and that he was not only very old but also extremely, almost unbelievably thin. Indeed, his clothes were little more than rags that hung like scraps from his body, and a gap in those rags revealed the horrifically exposed ribs that seemed almost to be breaking through his skin.

"Who is this?" Timothy asked. "I don't recognize him."

"Neither do I," Matheson replied, before crouching in front of the man. "Sir! You there, are you from round here? Why are you out in such awful weather? Haven't you heard that this storm is liable to get worse before it gets better?"

He waited, and above the sound of rain bashing the ground all around he heard the faintest of groans. This man – who barely seemed to be a man at all now – was clearly almost too weak to even raise his head. A moment later, Matheson saw thick cuts on the side of the man's neck, as if something had gouged deep scratches into his flesh. The wounds themselves were partially healed, although some of the scratches appeared to be much older than others, almost as if they had been occurring regularly for quite some time.

"How old is this poor bastard?" Timothy asked. "I'd wager he's almost a hundred!"

"I'd wager that you're right," Matheson said, as the old man finally managed to raise his head. "Yet there is something about him that I recognize."

"You think you've seen him before?"

"No," Matheson replied, lost in thought for a moment, "it is more that he reminds me of someone. His eyes, do they not seem somehow familiar to you?"

The old man opened his mouth and let out a faint, pained gasp. His whitened eyes, meanwhile, blinked a couple of times as rain ran down his face, and a few seconds later he reached forward with a trembling hand and grabbed Matheson's arm, squeezing tight as if he was trying desperately to make an impression.

"Where is she?" the man groaned. "Please... where is Patience?"

***

"This weather is so boring," Anne Purkiss said as she stood on tiptoes and stared out the window. Rain covered the glass in thick streams, driven by the wind and obscuring any proper view of the yard. "I want to go outside."

"Not in this weather, you can't," Patience Purkiss replied as she stood drying some plates over by the kitchen counter. Well into her seventies now, she winced a little at some pain in her joints, before setting one of the plates down and turning to look over at her granddaughter. "Anne, if you have too much time on your hands, I can easily find you a job to do."

"No!" Anne gasped, turning to her, as if this was the most horrible idea in all the world.

"Your grandfather might like to hear that you've been hard at work," Patience added with a faint smile. "After all, he's been out working hard all day despite the rain. Most people have. The world doesn't stop just because of some bad weather."

"But I might drown in all that rain," Anne pointed out.

"I'm not sure that such a thing is possible."

"I bet it is," Anne continued. "There's so much rain out there, I bet there's even more rain in the air than air itself." She furrowed her brow. "If you know what I mean."

"Why don't you go to the back of the house and sort through your grandfather's irons?" Patience asked, keen to find something for the girl to do. "You're eleven years old now, so I don't think they should be too heavy for you. And don't give me that doubting expression, young lady. By the time I was your age, I was going up and down chimneys in London, so you're certainly old enough to learn the meaning of hard work."

"Do you think it's fair, though," Anne replied, "to put a child to hard labor?"

"Where did you even hear those words?" Patience muttered. "Sometimes I wonder whether you're too clever for your own good."

"I don't think I am," Anne told her, before holding her arms out, "but I have very weak arms and I'm worried that if I try to lift Grandfather's irons, they might snap off."

"Your arms will *not* snap off."

"How can you be sure?"

"Fine," Patience said, unable to hide a sense of exhaustion, "your grandfather will just have to sort his own irons out. But you can't spend the rest of the day getting under my feet, for I have far too much to do around the house, not to mention out in the yard. Would you perhaps like to go and keep the horses company?"

"Can I?" Anne asked excitedly.

"So long as you don't bother them too much, and are careful," Patience replied as her granddaughter raced to the door. "Try not to overexcite them, though, for they have been rather sedentary over the past few days and they're liable to spook. Your grandfather has been delaying taking them out -"

"In case they drown in the rain?"

"No," Patience sighed, "but they don't like getting too wet and cold. I think they -"

"Somebody's here!" Anne called out.

Turning, Patience was about to ask her what she meant, but at that moment she spotted a figure hurrying across the yard. Unable to think of who might be calling on such a bad day, she took a moment to wipe her hands and then she crossed the kitchen and pulled the door open, just in time to find herself face-to-face with the rather soaked-looking gentleman who sometimes assisted her husband in making deliveries.

"Mr. Crowther?" she asked cautiously. "My husband is out at the moment, but -"

"It's not your husband I've come to see," Matheson Crowther said, sounding a little breathless. He looked down at Anne for a moment, and then back up at Patience. "I'm terribly sorry to disturb you, especially on a matter such as this, and particularly when the weather is so bad."

"What can I help you with, Mr. Crowther?" she replied.

"Something has come up," Matheson said cautiously. "Timothy and I found an elderly gentleman in the street earlier. We've taken him to the inn while we wait for a doctor, but he's very frail and sick and... I know this might come as a shock to you, Mrs. Purkiss, but I think the gentleman in question might be your father. I think it might be Samuel Butler."

Patience opened her mouth to reply, before hesitating for a few seconds. Reaching down, she instinctively touched the front of her dress, directly above the spot where – fifty-three years earlier – a knife had been forced into her belly and then twisted through her gut.

CHAPTER TWO

"HE'S NOT LONG FOR this world," one of the men at the bar muttered as he sat hunched over his ale. "Mark my words, that man -"

"Quiet!" the barman hissed, nudging his customer's arm. "He'll hear you!"

"I doubt he can hear much of anything these days," the man said, rolling his eyes. "Did you see the state of him when they carried him inside? I've seen corpses that looked more alive."

Over by the window, two tables had been hurriedly pushed together and the old man had been laid out on some old sheets. Every attempt had been made to give him some comfort, although in truth those gathered in the inn were fairly sure that little could be done. The man appeared to be drifting in and out of consciousness, occasionally letting out a faint groan but never quite managing to turn those groans into fully-formed words.

The landlord's wife was sometimes mopping his sweaty brow, partly because she felt it might help and partly because she simply believed that she needed to try something. Nevertheless, as she checked his pulse, she couldn't help but wonder whether death might be a greater mercy.

"Is it really him?" the man at the bar asked, leaning forward. "I mean... it can't be, can it?"

"There aren't many left around who ever met him," the barman replied, and he too lowered his voice and moved closer. "Even for those who might have done, so much time has passed."

"Wouldn't he be almost a hundred years old by now?"

"Aye, close enough. In his nineties, at least. Then again, some families have that in them."

"And what of his employer?"

"It's said that a man was sent from London some years ago, but that he took fright and ran from that house and no more attempts were made. Sounds like a strange way to run a business, although I suppose if the fright turned out to be big enough..."

His voice trailed off, and after a few seconds

he let out a long, slow sigh that suggested he had no more answers.

"This is a difficult story to get my head around," the man at the bar muttered. "But do you think, do you really truly believe, that the man over there on those tables is Samuel Butler of Hadlow House? I just can't get my head around the idea that after all this time, he just staggered into the village like that. Why would he do such a thing?"

"I don't see that it matters what I believe," the barman pointed out, rolling his eyes. "All I'll say is that, if that truly *is* Samuel Butler, then a few people in this village are going to have to make some decisions. It's all well and good to ignore a problem for year upon year, but eventually such problems fester for too long and they have to be looked into." He glanced over at the other end of the room, where two strangers had been conferring quietly in the corner snug for several hours now. "I'm more concerned about those two," he added. "Call me suspicious, but I don't much like it when strangers come to the area and keep themselves to themselves."

"Do you think they're up to no good?"

"Oh, I'm certain that they're up to no good," the landlord replied. "The question is... what kind of 'no good' are they up to?"

***

"When you said that we needed to get out of London and keep our heads down," Thomas Vowles said, sitting in the snug and keeping his voice low, "I didn't realize you meant that we'd be coming to the outright most peculiar village in all of England."

"Didn't you notice already?" his companion, George Jones, replied. "*All* the villages in England are peculiar. If you ask me, there's something about this country that breeds strangeness."

"So how long are we going to stop here for?" Thomas asked. "Every day we're in this wretched country is another day that we can't set sail and help our brothers back home."

"We'll help them in our own way," George told him firmly, "or have you forgotten exactly what we collected the other day?"

"I'm not sure that this is a good idea," Thomas muttered. "The British are angry enough already. If we go ahead with your plan, we'll be striking at the very heart of everything they hold dear. The consequences, if we get caught -"

"We won't get caught," George said, cutting him off.

"You can't promise that. They'll have our

heads on pikes!"

"We won't get caught," George continued, "because I'll have it all worked out perfectly. That's why we came down this way, remember? We just need to find somewhere we can stay for a little while, just until I've got everything ready." He glanced around, but nobody seemed to be paying him or his associate very much attention. "London's too crowded," he added, "but these villages are perfect. In case you haven't noticed, all the people we've encountered here are complete halfwits."

"I guessed that when they laid that fellow out on the table over there," Thomas said. "What do you think's wrong with him, anyway?"

"How should I know? The point is, these are simple folk who barely notice a thing. There's more intelligence and sophistication in my little finger than there is in all the people of Cattleford combined."

"Cattleford?"

"Isn't that the name of this wretched village? Caggleford? Cobbleford? Something like that?"

"I still don't like it," Thomas told him. "All it takes is one wrong move, and we'll be exposed. Where exactly do you think we can stay while we sort all of this out? Anyone who lets us rent rooms is going to want to know who we are and why we're here."

"We'll lie to them."

"I don't think it'll be as easy as you're suggesting," Thomas said, before leaning closer. "You're talking about blowing up the King of England," he continued. "That's treason!"

"It's a lesson he'll learn well," George replied. "Perhaps this will teach all the English to cease their infernal meddling in our affairs back home. The Americas aren't destined to forever remain a docile little colony of these old-fashioned idiots. We're going to be free, whether they like it or not!"

"I wish we had news," Thomas murmured. "I should like to know whether or not the first battle has been fought, and if so, who is the victor."

"The first battle will most certainly have been fought by now," George told him, "and I promise you that those British buffoons will have been licked and kicked back as far as the sea. They think they can do whatever they want with all their dominions, but their time is coming to an end. Mark my words, before this century is over we'll see a free America that governs itself, and we'll laugh as the British fade away into obscurity. Now, let's have no more talk of doubt, instead let's focus on the task at hand. We have what we need, we just need to find somewhere safe for a week or two."

"That's easier said than done."

"That fellow over there makes me feel worse by the minute," George said, glancing toward the table where the landlord's wife continued to tend to the stricken man. "Why must he keep gasping and puffing like that? If I were in such a state, I'm sure I'd have given up fighting by now. I'd rather die than linger like some old dog."

"You might get your chance," Thomas told him. "Besides, dying like a dog's better than being hung."

"No-one's getting hung," George replied, rolling his eyes as he turned to him again. "Will you just let me work on the plan? I promise you, we'll both be perfectly fine so long as we maintain a little discipline. The ones who fail, and who get hung or worse, are the ones who don't stick together. We're going to wait around in this little dump and find somewhere to stay, and then once we're ready to make our move we'll head back up to London and make sure the English realize that they're not even safe at home. Let me tell you something, God won't be saving any kings when we're done."

Hearing a creaking sound, he turned to look across the dimly-lit bar just in time to see a woman entering the inn. The woman stopped in the doorway, as if she was frozen in fear, and George kept his eyes on her for a few seconds before turning back to his associate.

"Well," he said with a grin, "looks like things are about to get interesting round here."

CHAPTER THREE

"IS IT..."

Standing just inside the inn's front door, Patience Purkiss stared at the motionless figure on the tables. Having rushed around the corner from her home, she'd barely had time to think about what she was going to witness. She was soaked from the rain and her hair was matted, but the sensation of wet clothes clinging to her skin was far from her mind. Instead, she saw the painfully frail-looking man and flinched as she thought back to the last time she was with him.

"I always knew that it wasn't your mother," he'd snarled on that day, leaning closer to her. *"And I will not let you, or anyone else, keep me away from her! Do you understand me? I will let*

no-one stand in my way!"

Again, she touched the front of her dress, remembering with vivid intensity the feeling of the knife's blade sliding into her gut.

And then he'd twisted the knife, causing even more damage.

"Father," she'd whispered as she began to lose consciousness. "Daniel. Someone... help me..."

"Father?" she whispered now, as she saw one of his hands moving slightly. "It can't be, can it? Surely there is some mistake here, this man cannot be my father, for my father would be nigh on ninety-eight years of age by this day." She tilted her head slightly. "Is someone playing a cruel joke?"

"It's no joke," Matheson Crowther said, standing just behind her. "He came into the village today under his own steam. I reckon he'd walked all the way from... well, from *that* place. Then he collapsed and we brought him in here, on account of not knowing where else to take him. We considered delivering him to you, Mrs. Purkiss, but we weren't sure that you'd want him."

She turned to Crowther.

"In the circumstances," he added cautiously. "After everything that happened, I mean."

She paused, before forcing herself to step across the room. Looking around, she saw a few figures at the bar staring at her, and two men in the far corner were observing as well. She felt as if she was being watched by almost everyone in the village, but as she reached the end of the two tables and looked down she let out a shocked gasp as she saw her father's painfully thin face staring up at her.

His eyes were almost entirely white, yet he seemed to be able to see at least a little, and a moment later he reached out with a bony hand and gripped her wrist.

After a few seconds of listening to him splutter, Patience realized that he seemed to be trying to say something. Her first thought was to turn and run away, yet she quickly reminded herself that – despite everything that had happened – this man was still her father, and that there had still been some good in him once. Slowly, and carefully, she lowered herself onto her knees so that she could look more directly into his eyes.

"It's me," she said, her voice thick with tension. "Perhaps the years have not been kind, but I'm sure you recognize me."

His lips parted and he managed another faint gasp.

"I thought you must be dead," she continued. "After that day, I never came out to the house again to disturb you. Daniel wanted to go and make you pay for what you did, but I told him not to. I almost died, Father. After you stabbed me, I lost so much blood, and by all accounts nine times out of ten I would never have recovered. That I managed was down entirely to Daniel, for he sat by me and tended to me and looked after me. A long time passed before I regained any of my strength, but with Daniel's help I eventually got to my feet again, and from that moment on I was determined to live my life."

She watched his eyes, and she saw milky orbs staring back at her.

"I don't even know why I'm telling you all of this," she added. "I doubt that you care. To tell the truth, Father, I assumed that you had died up at that house, that the woman there had finished you off. Can it be true, however, that you have survived for all this time? On what? *With* what? I have made sure that everyone knew to keep well away from that cursed place, for I believed it had become your tomb."

He managed another gasp, but his breaths seemed more rapid now, as if he was becoming agitated.

"You left me to die," she said softly. "I still remember the moment you walked out of that room. You never looked back, you never returned to check whether or not I had survived the grievous injury you gave to me. What were you doing instead, Father? How have you spent the past half a century? Have you merely been locked away in that house, surviving alongside that woman, that thing that haunts the rooms of Hadlow House? Is that what had brought you to this low point? If so, why are you here now? What -"

"I'm sorry..." he whispered.

She hesitated, before tilting her head slightly.

"Patience," he continued, his voice cracking with dry pain, "I should... I should never have... returned to that place..."

"But you did return," she pointed out.

"I was a fool," he told her. "I tried to leave so many times since, but she always..."

Now his voice trailed off, and his eyes flickered as he fought against the fear that seemed to be on the verge of consuming him.

"I finally got away," he gasped. "Patience, please, don't let... anyone... go there."

"Hadlow House should be burned to the ground," she told him.

"No!" he stammered, as if the idea was horrifying. "That would mean getting close to the place! She becomes stronger, Patience! Just leave it, treat it as if it does not exist and..."

He hesitated, before trying to reach toward her.

"Forgive me," he said softly.

"I do not believe that I can," she replied, as tears began to fill her eyes. "Not after what you did to me, Father. Not only did you drive that knife into my body, but you twisted it so that it would do the most damage. Even after the doctor saw me, I lay hovering between life and death for so long, torn by the knowledge that my own father had done such a thing to me yet still hoping that you would return, that you would see what you had done and that you would care. Daniel told me to focus on my own life, and eventually I did, and for all these years I pretended to myself that I did not care what had happened to you, but..."

As tears began to roll down her cheeks, she looked into his white eyes and tried to spot some trace of the humanity she remembered, of the father she had once loved.

"Don't go back," he gasped finally. "Just promise me that, Patience. I am going now to Hell, but you must not... ever... go back to that place..."

She hesitated, and then she opened her mouth to reply to him, and then – as a sense of dread filled her heart – she realized that he had stopped breathing.

Reaching out, she checked for a pulse but found none. Her first thought was that she could perhaps try to make him breathe again, that she might prolong his life for a few more minutes, but deep down she knew that there was no point. He was gone, and as she watched his dead eyes she found herself wondering whether he had been right in his estimation. Was he now, as he had predicted, entering the gates of Hell? Despite everything he had done to her, she preferred to think that he had perhaps found some peace, and after a moment she got to her feet and took a deep breath, before carefully closing the old man's eyes.

"You heard him," she said, her voice brittle with shock as she looked at the few gathered souls in the inn. "I know you all heard him. That house passes to me now, no doubt, and I want no-one to go near it ever again. No man, woman or child is to go within sight of Hadlow House. Is that understood?"

She turned and looked the other way. Shocked, gawping faces stared back at her, but Patience was filled with a growing sense of determination.

"I shall have a barrier erected to confirm the point," she added. "Please, let my father's body rest here for a few hours more, while I arrange for him to be taken away and given a proper burial, and then..."

Feeling a growing sense of horror, and aware now that she was going to burst into tears soon, she realized that she desperately needed to get out of public sight.

"That is all," she stammered, before turning and hurrying out of the room, heading out of the inn and leaving her father's body behind. "I'm sorry, but... that is all."

CHAPTER FOUR

"BUT WHERE ARE WE going?" Thomas asked breathlessly a few minutes later, as he hurried out of the inn and followed his companion along the narrow street. Rain was still crashing down. "Don't we need a plan?"

"We have a plan," George said firmly, not even bothering to look back at him. "Or, rather, *I* have a plan."

"But what is it?"

"Did you not hear a word of what just happened in that place?" George replied, stopping and turning to him so suddenly that Thomas almost slammed straight into him. Both men were already drenched by the storm. "Did you not listen to that hysterical woman? She spoke of a place, some Hadlow House, that we now know to be empty and abandoned. It is somewhere on the outskirts of the village, I'd wager, and it's absolutely perfect for our needs."

"What needs?"

"Sometimes I believe you to be simple in the head," George continued with a sigh. "We have need of a place where we can stop and take stock. A place where we can rest. A place where we will not be disturbed as we work toward our goal. Do you not see how this Hadlow House place can be useful to us? We know, for a fact, that nobody is going to go out there!"

"Alright," Thomas replied, "now I believe I understand, but we still have to discover the place."

"That will be easy enough," George told him. "Haven't you noticed that this entire village is filled with gossip and rumor? Why, we need only to speak to some passerby and I'm sure we'll have our directions to that house, if only because they'll want us to avoid it like the plague." He placed a hand on his friend's shoulder. "The Lord is smiling upon us and wants us to have this refuge, Thomas," he added. "I confess that I was worried before, but this opportunity has fallen into our laps and I cannot help but think divine grace is involved."

"That can only protect us for so long."

"It's a sign, however, and some men go to war with less. Indeed, with each passing day I feel more and more certain that we are being directed to achieve something great. In fact, I would go so far as to suggest that by our actions we are going to change the world."

"Shouldn't we ask a few more questions first?" Thomas said cautiously. "That man in the inn, the one who died just a moment ago, seemed to be in a state of terrible -"

"Old men died every minute of every hour of every day of the year," George replied firmly. "I'm not going to let that stop us. Trust me, Thomas. It is not just a matter of luck, that this house is available to us. I truly believe that the Lord is guiding us there, so that we can execute our plan! Now go and fetch the horse and cart. We do not have a moment to lose!"

***

Several hours later, the two men led their horse and cart along a rough, overgrown road that meandered through a thick section of forest beyond the edge of Cobblefield.

"Are you sure this is the right way?" Thomas asked, having to once again twist to avoid stinging nettles. Rain was battering the trees all around them, creating a loud hissing sound that seemed almost to be warning them to turn back. "It seems less like a road and more like a dirt track." He looked down at his feet, which had almost sunk into the mud. "There's a hole in my left boot," he added mournfully.

"I told you, I asked in the village and I was told that this is most assuredly the route to this Hadlow House place."

"But -"

"And rest assured, I was clever in how I went about the questions," George continued. "I did not ask the fellow outside the butcher's shop how to get to Hadlow House, for that would most certainly have caused questions to arise. No, I told him that I wanted to make sure that I *avoid* Hadlow House at all costs, and the fat little fellow was only too keen to tell me exactly which way not to go."

"I see," Thomas said, still unable to muster much enthusiasm.

"It would seem that this particular house has gained something of a reputation over the years," George told him. "You know what these little English places are like, they're full of fear and superstition. Why, I got the feeling that most of the people in Cobblefield would be happy if Hadlow House disappeared entirely off the face of the land, which is perfect for our needs."

"It is?"

"Because no-one will come out here and disturb us. You heard that madwoman back at the inn, she warned everyone to stay away. This is perfect!"

"If you say so, but -"

"There!"

Hurrying on ahead, George reached the edge of a somewhat rough clearing, and he stopped as he saw a wall with a large metal gate about twenty feet further on. Beyond that gate – which had been left wide open – there stood a dark-looking house that seemed somehow to be in the shadows of the nearby trees. The entire scene was strangely quiet, as if all the local wildlife had withdrawn from the area, but George couldn't help smiling as he looked around and saw that there was no sign of anyone at all.

"It's *better* than perfect," he said under his breath.

"Hadlow House," Thomas replied, reading from the iron sign above the gate. "At least we know we're at the right place."

"Of course we're at the right place," George said, stepping over to the gate and looking through into the wildly unkempt garden. "I don't know who that man was who died at the inn earlier, but it's clear that he carried out precious little work to look after the property. Why, it looks almost abandoned."

"There's a stranger atmosphere here," Thomas pointed out, leading the horse and cart over to him. "Can't you feel it? The air feels cold, somehow."

"You are a man of little imagination,"

George said, turning to him, "but boundless fear. Please, tell me that you have not succumbed to the same superstitions that have given us this fortuitous gift in the first place."

"I don't like the look of it," Thomas replied, peering past him and seeing that the house's front door had been left open and partially off its hinges. He stared at the darkness within for a moment, although he could make out nothing more than – perhaps – the faintest hint of the start of a staircase. "A house like this is not abandoned unless there is a very good reason."

"Houses like this are abandoned all the time," George told him. "I can think of a hundred and one reasons, just off the top of my head, why the place has been left in such a state. That old man clearly could not keep the place in a fit state, and evidently no-one else has any interest. Eventually someone *will* come and make the place their own, but for now it will do us just fine, since we need it for barely a week. If that."

He waited for a reply, and after a few seconds he smiled as he saw the continued fear in the face of his associate.

"I want you to tether the horse and feed him," he explained with a sigh. "Do you think you can manage that, Thomas? It's a rather simple task, it should be manageable."

"Where should I tether him?"

"Just find a post. I'm sure there must be one around somewhere. Make sure that the beast is secure, and then start unloading the cart."

"Unloading it? Why?"

"I worry that bad weather could spoil our cargo," George replied. "We have worked too hard, and taken too many risks, to let the elements have their say." He looked up at the sky. "You know what British weather is like, a sunny spell is no guarantee that later there will not be a thunderstorm. Certain modifications that I have made to the cargo, to increase its lifespan, have left it unusually vulnerable to rain." He glanced at Thomas again and saw the fear in the man's eyes. "It's perfectly stable," he added with a sigh. "I swear, you are a fellow who can conjure up concerns about any matter under the sun. Please try to leave the thinking to me, and just get on with the tasks you've been set. Do you think you can manage that?"

"I'll do my best," Thomas muttered, turning to look at the cart, where the cargo lay strapped down under several large sheets.

"And I shall investigate this house," George replied, setting off across the overgrown garden, striding toward the open front door with enthusiasm. "That foolish old man's bad luck is our gain. I must tell you, Thomas, that I have a very good feeling about this place!"

CHAPTER FIVE

"THE HORSE IS TIED," Thomas said as he made his way to the front door of Hadlow House and looked inside. Rain was dripping from the frame. "He seems a little anxious. I know not why, but I'm sure he'll settle soon. But I have to ask, when you asked me to unload the cart, where exactly did you mean that I am to put everything?"

He waited, but he heard no reply. As his eyes adjusted to the gloom, he saw the staircase rising up toward the top floor of the house, and he looked across the hallway and saw various open doors leading to different rooms. He was once again struck by a decidedly chilly atmosphere, but this time he reminded himself that he would gain no favors with George if he gave voice to his concerns, so instead he stepped into the house.

Almost immediately, a floorboard at the foot of the staircase welcomed him by creaking loudly beneath his left foot.

"George?" he called out. "Where am I meant to place the cargo, exactly?"

Still hearing no reply, he looked around again. One of the nearby doors had been left hanging off its hinges, and when he walked over to take a closer look he saw that the next room was a rather poky little place with a large, cold fireplace on one wall. There was no sign of life, although a moment later – looking down at the floor – he spotted a smattering of ash that had been left on the boards. Reasoning that this was of no concern, he walked over to another door and looked through into what appeared to be some kind of study, complete with books on the shelves and an empty chair that had been positioned in one of the corners.

"Who would live in such a wretched, dark house?" he muttered to himself, before stepping out once more across the hallway. Once again, the loose board near the bottom of the stairs groaned briefly beneath his weight. "I cannot fathom the choices that some people make."

Stopping again, he looked along the corridor. He had seen George entering the house earlier, of that he was certain, yet now there was no sign whatsoever of the other man.

"Where should I set the cargo down?" he

asked loudly, trying to hide the fact that he felt a little irritated by the lack of specific instructions. "George? I know you are here, so can you at least answer me?"

Again he waited, and a moment later he heard a bumping sound coming from somewhere upstairs. He looked up at the ceiling, and sure enough he quickly realized that George was up there somewhere.

"Come and see this!" George called out. "Thomas, hurry! You won't believe what I've found!"

***

"I thought this to be a fairly new house," Thomas said as he made his way to one of the upstairs rooms at the front of the house, "but it seems to be falling apart."

Stopping in the doorway, he looked into the room and saw an old bed in the corner. The room was a mess in general, with dirty sheets strewn across the floor, and there was even a hole in the wall just above the fireplace. A moment later he spotted George over by one of the other walls, and he made his way over to see what his associate had discovered. Water was dripping steadily from a small leak high above.

"This house must have been inhabited by a

true madman," George pointed out as he pointed at the various carved marks on the wall's wooden panel. "See here, and here. I can scarcely make any of it out, but he seems to have been writing the most unfortunate things over and over again."

"Help me," Thomas read from one section of the wall. "Save me. Forgive me."

"And those phrases are repeated here," George continued, pointing at a different section, "and here, and also over here. The writing is different, however, and some of the carvings appear to be much older than the others."

"So the old fellow was prone to writing on the walls of the house," Thomas suggested. "I have heard of such things happening before, but only in asylums."

"Indeed, but did he not mark you as perhaps weak in the head?" George asked, turning to him. "I assumed he was merely old, but now I fear that he might have been entirely insane. In which case, if he lived here all alone for some time, he appears to have descended into his own little world of madness."

Turning and looking around the room, Thomas had to admit that the place had all the trappings of a hospital room. Indeed, a moment later, he walked to the door and pulled it shut a little, and at that moment he spotted what appeared to be thick claw marks all around the handle and the lock.

"It's almost as if he was trapped in here at some point," he observed. "You don't think it's possible that he was kept here as a prisoner, do you?"

"I see nothing to support that claim," George told him, "but I understand your point." He walked over to the bed and looked down at the sheets, which bore various stains. "The air is rich with a fusty smell, and I see signs that the man soiled himself without even rising from this wretched spot. I hardly dare to imagine what his existence must have been like between these four walls, but from everything we witnessed in the village, I doubt that the man left very much."

"What was his name again?" Thomas asked. "Samuel something?"

"Samuel Butler," George replied, "and -"

Suddenly a loud bang rang out from elsewhere in the house. The two men looked at one another for a moment, both worried, and then George hurried out onto the landing. He looked around, concerned that at any moment he might spot another intruder, and then he heard the bang again – this time, the noise was most certainly coming from one of the other bedrooms. Hurrying over, he looked through into the room, and to his relief he was just in time to see an open window banging shut again in a gentle breeze.

"That's a relief," he muttered, heading over and pulling the window shut, then securing the latch. "I would not like to meet anyone else here."

"How do you know we will not?" Thomas asked, having followed him through.

"You heard that woman at the inn," George replied, turning to him. "No-one is to come near this place. We need only a few days, perhaps, for me to make sure that our plan is perfect, and then we will be gone. After that, it matters not who comes or does not come to the place." He looked around the room for a moment, and his face bore a very obvious sign of disgust. "If the house is truly left alone, as the lady wished, then I daresay it will collapse as soon as the next stiff breeze comes along. It doesn't seem to have been built in a very sturdy manner."

"You said you wanted me to unload the cart in case of a storm," Thomas replied, "but I don't know where to put the cargo."

"Bring it in here."

"In here?" he said incredulously, as if the idea was completely out of the question. "Are you serious?"

"I do not want it to get wet any more than is necessary," George told him, "and besides, it will be perfectly safe if you put it in one of the downstairs rooms. The one on the right, as you enter, should be fine. Remember, I have made modifications to the cargo that should make it much more secure. Unless you intend to light it on fire, I rather think that there is no danger."

"I'm not going to argue with you," Thomas said, turning and heading back across the landing. "I've learned better than to do that. Still, if there's one thing that appeals less than hanging, it's getting myself blown into a thousand pieces."

"You'll be just fine," George told him. "I have every faith in you."

"Oh, that's just wonderful," Thomas sighed, trudging down to the hallway and then stopped at the front door for a moment.

Looking out across the garden, he spotted an old oak tree near the fence. Something about this oak tree caught his attention for a few seconds, and he found himself wondering whether the tree had been standing since long before the house had ever been built. At least now that he was facing the garden, he no longer had to put up with the rather foul smell that filled the house, although after a moment he heard footsteps coming from somewhere over his shoulder and he turned to glance back at George.

"If you -"

Stopping suddenly, he realized that there was no sign of George at all. The footsteps had seemed to come from the far end of the hallway, perhaps from the room at the rear of the house, yet a moment later he heard the unmistakable sound of George still exploring the rooms upstairs. After waiting for a few seconds, just to make sure that the footsteps didn't return, Thomas told himself that he must simply have been mistaken. Instead of worrying about some vague sound, then, he stepped out of the house and began to make his way toward the cart.

"This had better be a good idea," he murmured under his breath. "I hope I haven't put my faith in the wrong cause."

CHAPTER SIX

STANDING IN HER BEDROOM at the house in Cobblefield, with the front of her dress pulled aside, Patience Purkiss stared at the twisted, knotted scars that criss-crossed her belly.

In that moment – not for the first time – she flinched as she recalled the sensation of the knife's tip penetrating her skin. How many times, over the years, had she relieved that awful injury? She didn't know the precise number, but she felt sure that it must be ten thousand or even a hundred thousand, and still she found herself thinking of it all over again. There had been something so firm and so deliberate about the way her father had stabbed her, and she still recalled the sense of her life draining away as she lay on the floor with blood pooling all around her.

"Grandmother?"

Startled, she quickly lowered the portion of fabric before turning to see Anne standing in the doorway.

"Grandmother?" Anne said cautiously. "Are you alright?"

"Perfectly," Patience lied, forcing a smile that she hoped would hide her sense of dismay. Heading across the room, she stepped out onto the landing and then pulled the bedroom door shut. "Are you still looking for something to do? If so, I can most certainly find a job for you."

"You seem different this afternoon," Anne said, looking up at her with an expression of slight bemusement. "Ever since you returned from wherever you went, you've been lost in your own world."

"I would caution against reading too much into small things," Patience said, taking the girl by the hand and leading her to the stairs. "A... small matter came up earlier, that's all, and it required my attention." They began to make their way down to the hall. "I have dealt with it, and that really is the end of things. I'm afraid life is really too busy for any of us to dwell on matters for too long."

"You're not sad, are you?"

Reaching the foot of the stairs, she turned to the girl and saw genuine concern and compassion in her eyes.

"You're growing up so fast," she said softly, before reaching out and tousling the hair on top of Anne's head. "I probably shouldn't say this, but every single day you remind me more and more of your dear mother."

"Is that a good thing?" Anne asked, before looking down at the rag-doll she was holding in her hands. "This belonged to her, didn't it?"

"That thing has been here longer than I have," Patience told her with a faint, sad smile. "Why, before your mother, it was owned by -"

Stopping herself just in time, she took a deep breath. Occasionally she caught herself, on the verge of saying something that might complicate matters, but she always managed to hold back. And then, saving her the trouble of thinking up some new topic of conversation, she turned just in time to see her husband hurrying in from the yard outside.

"Patience?" Daniel said, stopping in the doorway, his face a picture of concern. "I just returned from the field and... is it true? What they say about your father, I mean. Did he come into the village this morning?"

***

"He will be buried the day after tomorrow in the graveyard," Patience said as they sat at the table in the kitchen, next to a window overlooking the yard where Anne was now playing. The storm had passed and sunshine had arrived to start drying the puddles of rain. "I secured him a spot close to where my mother is buried. I thought that seemed... appropriate, despite everything that happened."

"That is all well and good," he replied, before reaching across the table and taking hold of her hands, "but it is not quite what I asked you." He looked deep into her eyes for a moment. "How are you feeling, Patience? What was it like to see him again after all this time?"

"It was unusual, I grant you that," she told him. "I had imagined such a meeting when I was younger, although as you know in recent years I had assumed that the chance had passed. There have been several men in his line who lived to a grand old age, but still, ninety-eight is remarkable. I just can't quite imagine how he can have survived all alone out there at the house for more than half a century, although..."

Her voice trailed off for a moment.

"Although," she added, turning to look out the window as tears once more filled her eyes, "we both know that he would not have been alone."

"You mustn't think of such things," Daniel told her.

"Yet I do, because they are important," she replied, trying to hold back yet more of the tears. "He went back to her, Daniel. He chose her over me, over his family, and he returned to that house and lived the rest of his life with that... creature. He chose to tie himself to a dark and evil spirit, even though he was under no illusion that it was my mother's ghost. What kind of man would do such a thing? What kind of man would try to kill his own daughter in his rush to get back there?"

"Patience..."

"I know you're going to tell me to put it out of my mind," she added, turning to him again, "but I'm sure you'll understand that I simply cannot. I have not set foot anywhere near that house in more than fifty years – in fifty-three years and two months and five days, to be precise – and I had thought that it was finally out of my mind, yet here I find myself contemplating it again, and I realize that it was never gone at all. I simply learned, for a while, to not think of it."

"Nothing has to change," he told her. "We'll make sure that your father has a proper burial, and then we'll get on with our lives."

"Anne -"

"Anne doesn't have to know anything," he added, before reaching across the table and taking hold of her hand. He squeezed tight, while watching her eyes to check her reaction. "She's a child," he pointed out, "and she wouldn't understand anything we told her."

"She deserves to know the truth," Patience

replied with a hint of desperation in her voice.

"When she's older."

"The longer we leave it, the harder it'll be for her." She turned and looked out the window, and she saw the little girl playing in the yard with her rag-doll near the horses. "Nobody deserves to have the truth hidden from them, Daniel. If I were in her position -"

"If you were in her position, you'd understand why we're doing this," he said firmly, giving her hand another squeeze. "We're her grandparents."

She opened her mouth to reply to him, before hesitating for a moment. Although she had managed for many years to focus on the here and now, the sight of her father laid out on the inn's tables had forced her to contemplate the past. As she watched Anne still playing in the yard, she was struck by the child's innocence, and she remembered that she too had been like that once, back in London when she'd been sent up chimneys, long before she had ever heard of Cobblefield or Hadlow House. She thought back to those days with her father and mother in their little house in the city; she loved her husband dearly, of course, and her life in Kent, but part of her wondered what things would have been like if she had never gone near that wretched house out beyond the edge of the village.

"That house took so much from me," she

whispered.

"We shall leave it alone," Daniel said as he let go of her hand and got to his feet. "I'll go out and secure it, and -"

"No!" she said firmly, turning to him. "You can't go near it!"

"I should at least check that the doors and windows are -"

"No, Daniel!" she snapped, getting to her feet. "Promise me that you'll never go near enough to see the place again. Let it rot! Trust me, I can feel in my heart that the evil spirit is still out there, and I know she'll hurt our family if she gets the chance."

"Patience -"

"Promise me!" she shouted, before taking a moment to try to regather her composure. "Promise me, Daniel," she added, a little more softly this time. "She killed my mother and my father. She wanted me too. I can't explain how I know, but I know... she will kill you if you go near that place."

He opened his mouth to reply, before shaking his head and letting out a heavy sigh.

"Fine," he muttered. "I suppose it makes little difference either way. Besides, I have much to do." He turned and headed toward the door. "I have been asked to assist in the search for two fugitives."

"Fugitives?"

"Two men suspected of treason." Reaching the doorway, he stopped and turned to her. "They are believed to have plotted against the king, in favor of the traitors who even now seek to seize the American colonies."

"Why would such men be in Cobblefield?" she asked.

"Hopefully they're not, or they just passed through," he told her. "Eventually someone will catch up to them, though," he continued, "and when they do, those two fiends will face a slow and painful death. If I were them, I'd find a place to hide away so that I might never be found."

CHAPTER SEVEN

"THERE HAS TO BE a better life than this," Thomas muttered under his breath as he hauled the last box off the back of the cart. Struggling with his grip, he immediately began to make his way toward the gate that led into the garden of Hadlow House. "I'm treated as if I'm nothing more than a pack animal."

He almost tripped on the uneven ground, but he somehow managed to keep going. After just a moment, spotting movement nearby, he turned and looked to his right, and he saw a figure nearby. A man wearing a white shirt was walking between the trees, and this man seemed to have only one arm. Within a few seconds the man was gone, however, and Thomas realized that he was not quite sure how this fellow had disappeared so quickly. He waited, watching in case the man appeared again, and then he turned and began to walk once more toward the house.

"And now I'm imagining things," he said with a sigh. "I wasn't cut out for this life. I should be back at home, with my feet up after an ordinary's day of work, not carrying this stuff around in the English countryside."

Glancing up, he saw that the afternoon sky was darker than usual. Until that moment he had assumed that the storm was now gone forever, yet the clouds appeared to be conspiring to have another try.

"Great," he added, "and now there looks to be a storm brewing. More of that wonderful English weather. I swear, the English seem cheerfully willing to endure such monstrous conditions, almost as if they realize it might be penance for the horrors they inflict upon the rest of the world."

A moment later George stepped out from the front of the house, looking over toward the far end of the garden.

"Did you see him too?" Thomas asked.

"Who do you mean?"

"There was some man out there," Thomas explained, "just walking through the forest. I was going to mention it to you, in case it's something to worry about, but he looked to be an old man and I believe he only had one arm. If you ask me, someone like that can't be much of a threat."

"I thought I spied something moving out there," George said, reaching down to check that his pistol was still at his waist. "It's probably nothing, but I should go and check."

"Do you need me to come with you?"

"No, I need you to finish storing the boxes. I fear bad weather is on the way and we really need to make sure that we're prepared." He made his way down the steps and out across the garden. "I won't be long, I just need to make certain that we haven't been noticed."

"What are you going to do if we have been?"

"Whatever it takes to guarantee silence," George replied with a faint smile. "Besides, I doubt anyone will miss some foolish old man who's probably just out doing a spot of poaching."

"More killing," Thomas said, turning and carrying the box into the house. "Sometimes I wonder just how many deaths are needed before we manage to prove our point. There are even times when I'm not sure this whole effort is worth all the pain and suffering we're bringing to the world."

***

A few minutes later, having set the last box down and rearranged the various items a little, Thomas stepped back and winced as he felt a sharp pain in the small of his back.

"There's a right royal smell in this place," he murmured, before heading to a door in the corner and looking through into what appeared to be some kind of storage room. "It's almost as if somebody left meat out to rot."

Satisfied that there was, at least, no meat in this particular part of the house, he stepped back into the study and made his way across the room. Reaching the hallway, he was about to go outside and attend to the horse when he heard a shuffling sound coming from somewhere nearby. Turning, he looked past the stairs and saw the open doorway that led into the kitchen, and he realized that the shuffling sound was continuing. His first thought was to call out to George, although he quickly reminded himself that George had gone out to check the forest. Realizing that he was alone, Thomas reached for his pistol and took it into his hand, and then he began to advance toward the kitchen.

"Hello?" he called out. "Is anybody there?"

As he passed another doorway, he glanced into the house's dining room. He saw a fairly long table, with empty chairs dotted all around, but there was no sign of anyone. Making his way toward the far end of the hall, he finally reached the door and looked into the large, long kitchen that spanned the entire rear of the house. The shuffling sound had stopped abruptly just a few seconds earlier, but Thomas still felt as if there was somehow a presence nearby, as if in some manner he could tell that he had arrived just a fraction of a second too late to see another person.

"Hello?" he said cautiously. "You should know that I'm armed."

He thought back to the man in the forest, and he wondered whether the fellow had somehow doubled back around.

"If there's anyone here," he continued, stepping into the kitchen as he told himself that he might yet prove his worth to George by capturing a spy, "then you'd better come out right now. Do you hear me? No good will come of skulking about."

He looked over at the counters and waited for a few seconds. Then, as he was about to turn, he felt something brush against his right elbow. Spinning around, he aimed the pistol and almost fired, only to hold back at the last second as he saw that there was nobody else in the room.

"Now what was that?" he asked, trying to not show that he was flustered. His heart was racing and he couldn't shake the feeling that someone was toying with his attention. "You won't prosper if you antagonize me, I'm..."

He hesitated as he tried to work out exactly how to make himself seem more impressive.

"I'm the master of this house, you see," he

lied, banking on the fact that an intruder would know no better. "I'm the new master of... Hodlore House or whatever it's called. The name's not important, what's important is that I'm in charge here and I don't want anyone creeping about." He adjusted his grip on the pistol, while his finger rested on the trigger. "I'm the master and -"

"Well," a woman's voice said suddenly behind him, "why didn't you say so?"

Startled, he turned and squeezed the trigger. Again he almost fired the pistol, only stopping himself at the very last second as he saw that it was aimed at the face of an older woman.

"Oh dear," the woman said, staring at the weapon, "that's rather unfortunate."

"Who..."

Thomas hesitated, before slowly lowering the pistol as he realized that there was no way that a mere woman could pose any threat whatsoever.

"You should have identified yourself as the new master immediately," the woman told him with a faint smile. "I was wondering who you might be, but I suppose I should have guessed. After all, you are a most striking gentleman and you have an air of authority about your person, a kind of natural command that I actually find to be exceedingly rare. Now that you say it, I can tell that you are indeed a born master."

"I am?" he asked, furrowing his brow.

"But where are my manners?" she added, stepping over to the table and pulling out one of the chairs, then gesturing for him to take a seat. "I'm afraid I have been terribly busy, but that is no excuse at all. It's just that nobody informed me that you were coming, and as you can tell the house is in rather a poor state. If I'd been told, I would of course have made sure that Hadlow House was impeccable for your arrival."

"Hadlow," he murmured. "Yes, that's right. That's the name of it."

"Please, take the weight off your feet," she said, gesturing again toward the chair, "and I shall see about finding something for you to eat. You must be hungry, of that I am quite sure."

"It has been a while since I ate well," he admitted cautiously.

"So sit," she continued with a generous smile, "and let me prepare a feast that you will not soon forget."

"I could do with some food," he muttered, stepping over to the chair and taking a seat. As soon as he had done so, he felt a great sense of relief. "I have been on my feet and carrying out orders for so long, I almost forget what it is like to actually have someone take care of me."

"No longer," she said soothingly, walking around him and heading to the counter.

"But there is nothing here," he pointed out.

"Where are you going to find food?"

"That's for me to worry about," she told him. "You must remember, my entire life has for some time been devoted to the masters of this house. First Mr. Hadlow himself, then his successor Mr. Butler, and now you."

"Is that the case?" he asked wearily, although he managed a faint smile. "So tell me, then, what exactly is your role?"

"My role?" She stopped and looked back at him, and now her smile grew. "Why, I am of course the housekeeper of this fine property. I am the woman who looks after Hadlow House and all those who live within its walls. That is my duty, and it is also my devotion. My name is Mrs. Baxter, but that sounds so formal, does it not? I would prefer it if you were to use my name." She paused for a moment. "And that is Frances, although I would be greatly honored if you would call me Fanny."

CHAPTER EIGHT

"HELLO?" GEORGE CALLED OUT as he stood in the forest, almost a mile from Hadlow House. Looking around, he saw no sign of life, but he could not yet quite calm his fears. "If there is anybody here, you should show yourself now."

He waited, and he couldn't shake the thought that he was perhaps shouting at shadows. Ever since he and Thomas had been betrayed in London and had fled under cover of darkness, he had been living on his wits, constantly worried that agents of the crown might yet catch up with him and make him face a traitor's death. He had reassured Thomas that no such thing could happen, of course, but those words had done little to calm his own doubts. Now, standing in a forest in a strange part of England that he knew poorly, George

Jones knew that at any moment his life might be brought to an abrupt and painful end.

A moment later, hearing a rustling sound, he turned and saw an elderly man stumbling between the trees. The sight seemed strangely incongruous, as if on some deep instinctive level he could already tell that this man did not belong.

"Halt!" George called out, raising his pistol. "Come no closer!"

"Oh, I'll come no closer to you, Sir," the man said, stopping between two trees and staring at him. "Not you, not such a fine gentleman."

"Who are you?" George asked, before noting that the man was indeed missing one of his arms. "Are you some peasant from the village?"

"From the village? You mean from Cobblefield, Sir?" The man hesitated, before slowly shaking his head. "No, Sir, I am nothing of the sort. I was brought here with my wife to serve our master."

"And who might that be?"

"Mr. Hadlow, of course."

"Hadlow?" George hesitated, while still aiming his pistol at the man. "Of Hadlow House?"

"Why, the one and the same," the man replied, tilting his head slightly and finally allowing himself a faint smile. "He was a good man, Sir, although he was laid low by bad luck and some poor judgment. I always thought -"

"Cease this prattling," George continued, interrupting him. "I don't care about some long-ago man who might have brought you here, I want to know why you are on this day wandering around in the forest so close to the house. Did someone put you up to it?"

"I beg your pardon?"

"Did someone send you out here?" George asked, and now his agitation was become more and more apparent. "Are you an agent of some force?"

"An agent of some force?" the man replied, clearly a little puzzled by the question. "Why, I'm not entirely sure what you mean, but I don't consider myself to be an agent of a force." He paused, before looking around at the trees. "I don't rightly know," he continued, "what I'm doing at this exact moment. Truth be told, Sir, I rather feel that I have been walking for quite some time and never quite arriving at where I aim to be. And the more I walk, the more I lose all sense of where I am going, except that I feel..."

He paused, letting his voice hang for a few seconds, before slowly turning to George again.

"I feel that I cannot go to where I am needed," he added darkly. "Tell me, have you seen my wife?"

"Your wife?" George asked incredulously. "Why would I have seen your wife?"

"Dear Fanny," the man continued, "is a

good woman, although I'd wager that she'd all tied up in knots now. I haven't seen her for so long, and while she might have her faults, the fact remains that she is my wife and I should be by her side. Yet I cannot go to her." He held his one hand up, staring at it as if there was something about its appearance that he couldn't quite believe, and then he looked down at the stump at the end of his other arm. "I rather fear," he whispered, "that I have become lost."

"What you have become is of no concern to me," George said through gritted teeth. "All I'm worried about is where you're going next."

"Me, Sir?" the man replied. "You don't need to worry about me, Sir. I -"

Suddenly George pulled the trigger, blasting him straight in the face. As the discharge from the pistol cleared, however, he saw to his horror that the man was still standing before him as if nothing had happened. After a moment, reaching up, the man touched his own face as if he was searching for some kind of damage or wound.

"How is this possible?" George whispered.

"I don't rightly know, Sir," the man stammered, "but I think..."

He hesitated, before lowering his hand.

"I think," he added, "that you really oughtn't to have done that, Sir."

George opened his mouth to reply, but in

that instant the man rushed at him. Startled, George stepped back and bumped against a tree, only to find that there was now no sign of the strange man at all. He looked around, convinced that the man must simply have ducked out of view, yet there was nothing left of him, as if he had simply vanished into thin air.

"This land is cursed!" he muttered, turning and hurrying back through the forest. "The sooner I get back to America, the better!"

***

By the time he got back to the garden of Hadlow House, George's mind was filled with doubt and fear. He'd hoped to calm his racing thoughts on the walk, but instead he'd found himself becoming more and more panicked until finally he stopped at the gate and tried to regather control of his senses.

"I shall not let that fool Thomas see me like this," he said firmly, determined to stop obsessing over the old man in the forest. "He was not real. He can't have been. I merely imagined the fellow."

He took a deep breath as he looked at the house, and after a few seconds he realized that he was perhaps starting to feel more like himself again. The afternoon was slowly turning into evening, bringing the first hints of darkness, and the sky above remained dark as if a storm might yet break at any moment. Having been preoccupied by his strange encounter in the forest, George had not yet given much thought to his plans for the night, but he knew that he had to be particularly cautious. The old man had been proof – if proof had ever been needed – that even in a dull little village like Cobblefield there was danger all around.

And danger, George knew, had to be avoided at all costs. He was not a coward, but he was also not a man who liked to waste time and energy dealing with unnecessary problems. Indeed, he had long since prided himself upon an ability to second-guess potential difficulties and nullify them before they took root.

"Fine," he said, taking another deep breath before marching toward the house. "There is no need to tell Thomas anything about what happened out there. He's enough of a nervous wreck already."

Realizing that he was talking to himself, which was something that often happened when he was experiencing great stress, he quickly resolved to stay quiet. Reaching the front door, he pushed it hard, only to find to his surprise that it would not open. He tried again, then for a third time, before taking a step back.

"What is that fool doing now?" he sighed, before starting to make his way around the house, determined to go to the back door. "That thing was barely even on its hinges when I left. He should know better than to interfere. Why, I've got a mind to -"

Suddenly, as he reached the corner, he almost walked straight into a woman who was coming the other way.

"I'm so sorry!" the woman gasped, taking a step back. "Oh, Sir, you must forgive me, but I didn't know that you were here."

"Who are you?" he asked angrily.

"I'm the housekeeper," she told him.

"What housekeeper?"

"The housekeeper of Hadlow House," she explained, as if the answer was exceedingly obvious. "I have been the housekeeper for many years and -"

"We haves no need of a housekeeper!" he snapped.

"Well, I'm afraid I rather come with the house these days," she replied. "Allow me to introduce myself, my name is -"

"I don't care about your name," he sneered, disgusted by the sight of her. "I have been gone barely over an hour, and already that fool Thomas has engaged a housekeeper? I thought I had the measure of his stupidity, but evidently he is exceptional when it comes to such matters."

"I'm not sure that's entirely fair, Sir," she said cautiously. "As I explained, I come with the house. In fact, with all due respect, I would say that it's rather difficult to get rid of me." She smiled, before looking around. "Indeed," she added softly, "this is the first time I have been outside for many years. I wasn't able to leave the property before, but now I seem to be able to advance a short distance."

"I do not care," George told her bluntly. "Not about you, and not about any of this." He hesitated, watching her with a growing sense of suspicion. "But what has Thomas told you?"

"Oh, nothing," she replied. "Barely anything at all."

"Is that right?" He paused, before stepping past her. "Wait here, while I check. I must -"

"Sir?"

Sighing, he stopped and turned to her.

"What now?" he asked, his voice filled with fury. "I am in no mood for -"

Before he could get another word out, Fanny swung an old metal shovel at him, slamming the sharp edge straight into the front of his face with a crunching blow. She tried to pull the shovel out as blood gushed from the wound, but she found that it was stuck for a few seconds until finally she gave it a twist. As soon as the metal slipped out of the deep cut on George's face, the spluttering man dropped to his knees and then keeled over onto the muddy ground.

CHAPTER NINE

"CHECKMATE," PATIENCE SAID AS she watched Anne moving the bishop across the chessboard. "Well, I must say, my darling, that you have beaten me again."

"You let me win," Anne replied with a giggle.

"I did not!"

"But you're so old," Anne pointed out. "How can you lose to me?"

"I've never been good at chess," Patience replied, getting to her feet and – at the same time – feeling a pain in her right knee. "You're a smart young lady," she added, "certainly smarter than me. You obviously take after your -"

Stopping just in time, she paused for a moment before forcing a smile.

"Well," she added, "that's quite enough chess for today. I have to admit, my brain is rather tired from trying to beat you. You put up a very good fight."

"For a girl," Anne said softly.

"For anyone," Patience told her, as she picked up a pair of scissors and thought of the flowers she needed to cut in the next room, "and never let -"

Suddenly she froze, and after a moment she stepped back and supported herself against the side of the dresser. As a sense of nausea and fear gripped her chest, she struggled to stay on her feet, and when she looked around she felt sure that great evil was approaching. Hurrying forward, she grabbed Anne and pulled her close, wrapping her arms around the girl to keep her protected even as she looked all around the room and tried to work out why she was filled with such terror. Deep down, however, she already knew that this awful sensation was coming from somewhere else.

"What's wrong?" Anne asked. "Is -"

"Quiet!" Patience hissed, pulling her even tighter. "I need to listen!"

"But why?"

"Just let me listen!" Patience said, as her sense of panic became stronger and stronger.

For the next few seconds, Patience could only look around the room and wait for catastrophe to strike. She felt absolutely certain that someone or something was approaching, and she quickly realized that she had only encountered this sensation once before. No matter how hard she tried to push the idea out of her thoughts, she couldn't shake the feeling that Fanny Baxter was about to appear in the room and rush at her and try to steal her granddaughter away.

"Grandma," Anne said, "you're -"

"Shut up!" Patience shouted, pulling her even closer until she couldn't hold her any tighter. "I'm trying to protect you!"

"But Grandma -"

"Shut up, Anne!" Patience screamed, and now sweat was pouring down her face. "You don't know what's happening, but I do! There's a horrible, nasty woman and I thought she was far away and that she was out of my life forever but now I can feel her coming closer and -"

"You're hurting me!"

Looking down, Patience was about to tell her – yet again – to be quiet, when she saw that not only was she holding the girl tightly by the throat but she also had the scissors open with their bladed edges starting to push against Anne's skin. After hesitating for a moment, horrified by the sight, Patience pulled away and let the scissors drop from her trembling hand.

"You were hurting me," Anne said, with

tears in her eyes. "Grandma, what's wrong with you?"

"Nothing," Patience said, and now the sense of Fanny's presence had begun to fade. "Nothing at all. Just stay here and be good." She paused, before picking the scissors up and rushing out of the room. "I need to go outside for a moment," she stammered. "I just... I need some air..."

***

Standing at the entrance to the yard, looking along the narrow street that led toward the south of the village, Patience finally felt as if she'd managed to get her breath back.

For the past few minutes, she'd been trying to convince herself that she'd been wrong, that she'd simply suffered a little wobble. After all, her father's sudden return after fifty years – and his death on those tables at the inn – had undoubtedly left her feeling more than a little unsteady, and she reasoned that this would be more than enough to bring the past floating back up into her thoughts. At the same time, the sensation in the house had been so strong that she couldn't shake a new sense of fear, and she was unable to quite convince herself that the whole thing had been in her mind.

What if Fanny Baxter had somehow reached out from the house and had managed to – albeit very briefly – slip into her thoughts?

She remembered the night she'd escaped from Hadlow House. She'd climbed up the chimney in one last, desperate attempt to secure her own freedom, and once outside she'd felt as if Fanny could never get to her again. Life on Cobblefield had felt safe, because she'd been quite sure that Fanny was confined by the walls of the house. Now she couldn't help but wonder whether she might have been wrong, whether Fanny had either always been able to reach further or had perhaps recently developed this new ability.

If that was the case, then what else might she be able to do? Would anyone in Cobblefield be safe?

"Can you..."

She paused, worried that by letting her fears out she might enable them to grow stronger. She watched as a young boy carried a dead pig toward the butcher's shop, and then – realizing that she alone – she looked up at the sky.

"Can you hear me?" she whispered. "Are you out there, Fanny?"

In her mind's eye, she saw the house again, standing all alone in its garden in that clearing in the forest. The late afternoon sky was starting to darken, so she thought of the low light glinting against all those dark windows, and of Fanny's cruel, angry face staring out at the world. She had thought of this image many times, yet somehow she had always been able to keep it from developing fully in her thoughts; now, however, the image of the house flooded every corner of her mind, filling her soul with the most powerful sense of dread possible, and all of this hatred and fear was focused on that simple image of the dead woman at the window. In that moment, standing at the edge of the yard in the center of the little village, Patience knew without any shred of doubt that Fanny Baxter's ghost was still at Hadlow House.

Still waiting.

"You won't get me," she whispered. "I don't care how hard you try, or how long you think you can wait, I will *never* set foot in that house again, and I will make sure that no-one from my family goes there either. Do you understand? You will never get any of us."

She heard no reply in her head, of course, but she felt the sense of Fanny's presence twisting and burning in the air, as if the dead woman was once again reaching out from the house. Patience knew that this was a fresh development, but she tried to stay strong and she reminded herself that even if Fanny could somehow reach out, her ghostly presence was still trapped at Hadlow House forever.

"Give up," she said under her breath now. "Forget about me. Forget about my family. Haunt that place if you want, but for as long as I have any say over the matter, you will not get anyone through the front door. The Wallaces deeded the house to my father, and that deed passes to me now, and I will keep every living soul away from you. Do you understand?"

"Good afternoon, Mrs. Purkiss," one of the men from the ironmongery said as he walked past. "Looks like rain soon."

Patience turned and looked at him. She stared for a moment before just about managing to smile, although she saw a hint of confusion on the man's face as he slowed his pace and looked back at her.

"Mrs. Purkiss?" he said cautiously. "Are you quite alright?"

"I'm perfectly fine, Andrew," she replied. "Thank you."

"But..."

He hesitated, looking down at her hands.

"You're bleeding," he added.

Following his gaze, she was surprised to see that she had clenched her fists tight shut with such strength that her fingernails had dug into the palms, cutting the skin. As soon as she un-clenched her fists, she felt a sharp pain in both hands and she saw the damaged ribbons of flesh.

"That's nothing," she told the man. "You're right about the rain, though. It'll be in the air soon. We'd best all get inside and take shelter."

Andrew nodded and walked on, leaving Patience once again alone in the street. She turned and looked past the buildings opposite, and she could just about see the tips of trees in the distance. She knew that those trees marked the start of the forest, and that further off in that forest Hadlow House was still waiting, and that the ghost of Fanny Baxter was waiting in that house.

"Goodbye, Fanny," she said through gritted teeth. "I know you're still there, but I shall never come to you. And I hope that one day you rot in Hell."

CHAPTER TEN

"THIS IS MOST DELICIOUS," Thomas said, sitting at the far end of the dining table in Hadlow House as he chewed on the wonderful serving of pork shoulder that had been placed on his plate. "I must admit, I didn't expect very much at all, Mrs. Baxter, but you have absolutely delivered."

He chewed for a moment longer, before looking along the table. There was no sign of anybody else; nor, when he looked through toward the hallway, did he spot the housekeeper or even hear her. He waited, chewing a little longer, and then he swallowed.

"Mrs. Baxter?"

Confused, he got to his feet and walked over to the doorway, where finally he saw her. She was standing at the open front door, staring out at the garden and seemingly lost in some kind of trance. Thomas waited, convinced that at any moment she would turn to her, and then he let out an involuntary burp.

"I'm terribly sorry," he muttered. "The truth is, I can't remember the last time I had a good, proper meal." Dabbing at the corners of his mouth with a handkerchief, he turned and looked back at the food on the table; there was still plenty to get through, and his appetite – although satisfied – was not so swollen that he was going to turn down the rest of the feast. "You are a most magnificent cook," he added. "I confess, you would seem to be an asset to this place."

He turned to her again, only to let out a shocked gasp as he found that she was now standing directly in front of him.

"I must apologize," she said calmly, "but I was lost in my own thoughts for a moment. I was just... thinking of an old friend who resides now in the village."

"Do you ever go to visit this friend?" Thomas asked, trying to make pleasant conversation.

"Visit?"

"Into the village," he continued, wondering why she found the question so unusual. "It's not that far to walk, is it? Indeed, when the weather is good, I can imagine that the walk might even be rather pleasant."

"Indeed, it most certainly can be," she replied cautiously, "but... no, I have not seen this particular friend for quite some time. I'm sure I shall, however. It's only a matter of waiting." She peered past him. "Do you have enough food there, Mr. Vowles? If you like, I can go to the kitchen and whip up some more. We have a small but very useful basement room that is just perfect for curing meats."

"I think that what is on the table will be quite -"

Before he could finish, Thomas let another burp.

"Quite satisfactory for now," he added, before wiping his mouth again. He turned to go back to his seat, before stopping and looking at Fanny again. "Although it is getting dark outside, and I'm sure that George will be back soon."

"George?"

"My associate. Mr. Jones."

"Of course," she replied with a polite smile and a brief nod. "Well, when he returns, there will certainly be enough for him to eat as well."

"He's going to be most surprised," Thomas said, burping yet again as he walked to the end of the table and retook his seat. "Actually, I wouldn't be surprised if he's out there foraging for scraps right now, completely unaware that when he returns there will be a feast for him to consume." He chuckled. "I can't wait to see his face."

"Please, enjoy the rest of your food," Fanny told him. "I shall be amply prepared to feed your Mr. Jones or anyone else who arrives at the house tonight." She paused for a moment, once again lost in thought. "I am always prepared for visitors."

***

Several minutes later, as he chewed the last mouthful of food, Thomas set his knife and fork down and sat back in the chair. The wooden legs heaved slightly beneath his weight, as if they had noticed some increased girth following his meal, but Thomas told himself that he more than deserved a moment of gluttony.

Placing his hands on his belly, he realized that he felt full and content for the first time in months.

"Our cause may be just," he said, to nobody in particular, as he stared at the empty chair at the dining table's far end, "and our goals noble, and the Lord might guide us in our work, but that doesn't mean it hasn't been hard from time to time and -"

Another large burp shook his body briefly.

"Well," he continued, "it's nice to be fed properly in the -"

Before he could finish, he realized that he

could hear an unusual sound. He fell silent and listened to what seemed to be a faint squelching noise, although the precise nature of this noise escaped him; he felt, after a moment, as if someone or something was perhaps stirring a spoon through some thick, bubbly liquid, or perhaps as if unseen hands were reaching deep into thick mud and rooting around for something. A few seconds later the sound changed, becoming more like a soft, minuscule chewing noise, although when he looked around he could see nothing that might explain such a thing.

He glanced toward the far end of the table and saw only another empty chair, with the bare and unused fireplace a little further back. At that moment he felt a shiver pass through his body, and as he hauled himself to his feet he made a mental note to ask Mrs. Baxter about arranging some heat.

"I had better -"

In that moment, he expressed a loud and rather vulgar fart from his backside.

"Oh dear," he said with a smile, amused by his own flatulence, "I *do* seem to have -"

He farted again.

"I must maintain some dignity here," he continued, before stepping around the table and starting to make his way toward the door. As he did so, however, he realized that the chewing sound was becoming louder, and he stopped again to listen; the sound persisted, seemingly coming from somewhere very close, and now he felt sure that something or someone was sucking on something and grinding it with their teeth.

He looked around, yet still he saw that he was alone in the room.

"Well," he said, "if -"

Suddenly he looked toward the window, and in that moment he spotted not only his own faint reflection in the glass, but also the reflection of a woman sitting at the table. He stared in horror, until the woman slowly turned to look at him. Stepping back, he bumped against the wall, knocking a vase from the dresser.

The vase smashed against the floor. Thomas looked down, and then he looked at the window again, and this time the woman was gone.

"Hello?" he stammered, even though he knew that her face must have been a trick of the light. She had looked younger than Mrs. Baxter, that much was clear, and her eyes had been filled with darkness.

He waited, and now he realized that not only was the younger woman gone, but the chewing sound had stopped and the room had fallen once more into silence.

"H... Hello?" he whispered.

Silence prevailed, and after a few seconds Thomas told himself that he had simply fallen prey to a surfeit of meat. He touched his belly, which felt a little round and distended, and then he looked at the broken vase and told himself that Mrs. Baxter would be only too pleased to clean up the mess.

"I think I might have a little rest," he murmured, stepping out into the hallway and lumbering over to the foot of the staircase, before stopping and listening out for some sign of the housekeeper. He took another step forward, and his right foot pressed down upon the loose, creaking floorboard near the door to the study. "Mrs. Baxter?" he called out. "If it's quite alright with you, I think I shall go upstairs and settle on one of the beds for a while, so that I am better able to digest that wonderful meal. Would you mind telling George... I mean, Mr. Jones... that I am napping and that there is no point disturbing me. I'm sure I'll be awake after a few hours, but if I sleep all through until morning..."

He paused for a moment, and he had to admit that he felt extremely tired.

"Well," he added, "that would not necessarily be such a bad thing, would it? A man deserves his rest, after all."

With that, he began to make his way up the stairs, although he felt so heavy that he had to grip the banister for support. He winced a couple of times too, but he forced himself to make the climb until finally he reached the landing. There, he looked around for a moment before picking one of the bedrooms at random and making his way through, and a few seconds later the door bumped shut behind him.

Down in the hallway, standing in the shadows by the front door as the sun continued to set outside, Fanny watched the stairs. She had been there for some time now, but Thomas had simply not noticed her. Now she stepped forward, walking serenely across the hallway and stopping at the door under the stairs. She looked around for a moment, and then – without opening the door – she simply stepped straight through it and disappeared entirely from view.

1775

CHAPTER ELEVEN

"I THINK GRANDMA LETS me win," Anne said as she sat at the dinner table at the house in the village. "I think I should start playing other people, to test."

"Is that right?" Daniel asked, smiling at the girl. "If you are challenging me to a game of chess, then I most certainly shall accept, although it's getting late now and you should go to bed after we've eaten. We can play tomorrow, perhaps, if I am able to find the time. You know, your great-grandfather – my own father – had a keen mind and could beat many men at chess. It is possible that you take after him."

"What about my mother?" Anne asked, and now there was a notably cautious tone to her voice. She seemed cautious, as if she didn't really want to ask the question at all. "Was *she* good at games like chess?"

"That's quite enough talk of such things," Patience said firmly. "Are you going to finish you supper, Anne, or are you not hungry?"

"Oh, I'm hungry," Anne replied, making a show of eating again. "I'm sorry, Grandma."

"You're back with us," Daniel said, watching his wife with just a hint of concern. "For the past few minutes, you seemed to be thinking of something else entirely."

"Do you have any idea how many tasks fall to a modern wife?" she asked. "I have to keep this place running all day while you're working."

"And I have always appreciated your efforts," he told her, "but today you seem a little different. I know that you have always tended to have such moments, yet you must forgive me if I am a little more attentive of late. If this change in your demeanor is on account of your father, then -"

"It has nothing to do with him," she said firmly, cutting him off. "That man was barely my father at all, not for these past fifty years. I don't know why you think I should feel anything at all now that the man is dead, but as far as I'm concerned he might as well have died all those years ago when he..."

She stopped herself just in time as she saw Anne staring at her with a somewhat confused expression.

"Anne," she continued, "if you've finished eating, which you seem to have done, then it might be time for you to excuse yourself from the table and perform your ablutions."

Anne opened her mouth to reply.

"And that's my final word on the matter," Patience added, fixing her with a firm stare that she hoped would get her point across. "In all seriousness, Anne, you're up later than usual and I'd very much like you to settle down now."

Although she was clearly not happy about the idea, Anne climbed off her chair and made her way out of the room, leaving Patience and her husband sitting in silence for a few seconds.

"Ablutions?" Daniel said finally, with a smile. "You certainly use some fancy words now and again, Patience."

"There's no harm in that," she replied, before sighing heavily. "I suppose I always felt rather inferior when I was a girl, and I though that learning fancy new words would make me appear more intelligent. But you're probably right, I shall always be a little chimney girl from London, shall I not?"

"Don't be so quick to dismiss yourself," he told her. "I've been in awe of you since the day we first met, Patience. You don't think I used to invite just any girl to meet me on the stone bridge back then, do you?"

"We should go to that bridge again," she suggested. "It has been too long."

"I agree with you," he replied, getting to his feet and walking around the table until he was behind her, then placing his hands on her shoulders. "I also think that you're so very tense, my dear. You have so many responsibilities, and I worry that you never have time to just sit back and relax. And no matter how many times you tell me that you're fine, I *know* that recent events with your father must have – at the very least – stirred up some old and very painful memories."

Patience sat thinking for a moment, staring into space as her mind once again drifted back to that awful day many years earlier. She felt as if a rush of memories might be about to swamp her entirely, and she was truly no longer sure than she could hold those memories back forever. At the same time, one particular point remained stuck in her mind, threatening to bring forth a hint of genuine bitterness.

"He chose her," she said finally.

"What -"

"Father chose Fanny Baxter," she continued, "over me. Over Mother, even. Over his entire family. We saved him, Daniel. Don't you remember? We saved him from her, yet he merely went back to her and then he stayed for half a century. What was he doing in that house for all those years?" She looked up at him. "Fifty years would be well over ten thousand days, would it not? What was my father doing in that house, with that woman, for more than ten thousand days and nights?"

"Sinking deeper and deeper into her world, it would appear," he told her. "But there's no -"

"You saw him," she added, before he could say another word. "He was so old and frail, he looked almost like a corpse even before he died. It's as if he forced himself to linger for just long enough to come into the village, but why was he allowed to leave the house? How did he finally escape?"

"We'll never know."

"What scares me," she continued, "is that Fanny's ghost realized that Father was about to die, and she sent him here as a kind of message."

"For who?"

"For me," she said firmly. "She wanted me to know that she's still out there. That she's still waiting."

"I fear that you're making this far more difficult for yourself than it needs to be."

"I sensed her, Daniel," she explained. "I don't know how, I can't really explain, but I sensed Fanny reaching out to me. Do you remember when we thought Father was saved from her, and he went back? I think she wants *me* to go back."

"You wouldn't actually do that, would you?"

"Of course not, but what if she keeps trying? What if she won't ever give up."

"She's alone," he pointed out, rubbing her shoulders from behind. "You have me, Patience, and I won't let anything happen to you. Or to Anne, before you start worrying about that as well. You might be right, Fanny might be waiting for you, or you might be wrong and she's simply haunting that place all by herself. Or she might even be gone, and -"

"She's not gone."

"If -"

"That house is to remain empty forever," she added, getting to her feet and turning to him. "Do you understand? It must be empty and abandoned."

"As you said earlier, we -"

"Let the whole world just pretend that it doesn't exist," she told him. "And if Fanny is still there, let her rot all alone forever." She paused for a moment. "Then again, it's only her soul that remains there. Her body is in the cemetery at St. Leonard's. I can't imagine whatever possessed someone to give her a proper burial, but what if we could do something to her bones that would get rid of her forever?"

"Now you're starting to worry me," he replied. "Patience, no-one is going to start digging up bones. Do you understand?"

"But -"

"No-one," he said firmly. "Listen to yourself for a moment and recognize that you are becoming hysterical. I have told you that we'll leave that house well alone, and that simple promise should be enough for you. I would even go and burn it to the ground, but -"

"No!"

"But I won't," he added, "because I know you don't want me or anyone else to go near the place."

"It's all one huge trap," she added, with tears in her eyes. "Do you see that, Daniel? Her malevolent, malignant spirit is waiting there and anyone who enters Hadlow House now will become her victim. I can't promise that the house will remain empty and untouched forever, but I *can* make sure that nothing happens while I am alive. And other than that, I can only pray that the Lord will take care of that wretched woman, and that soon she will no longer be able to trouble anyone alive or dead."

"Patience..."

He hesitated, before stepping closer and kissing her on the forehead, and then he gently tapped her nose.

"You're not taking me seriously," she said with a sigh.

"I am," he replied, "and I shall honor your wishes. I promise. You have no need to show further concern, my darling. I love you and I will keep you and our family safe forever. Do you understand that? I can only implore you to forget about Hadlow House and about Fanny Baxter, and to focus on the tasks at hand. Tomorrow we shall bury your father in the churchyard, and then we must try to get on with our lives. Do you think you can do that?"

"Perhaps," she said cautiously. "With you by my side, at least."

"I shall *always* be by your side," he said, before leaning closer and kissing her tenderly on the cheek. "You must have no fear in that regard."

CHAPTER TWELVE

"WHAT?"

Startled, Thomas sat up suddenly and found himself utterly lost and confused. Looking around the gloomy room, with just a hint of light framing the window as the sun finished setting in the distance, he was momentarily unsure of his whereabouts, before finally he felt his full belly and realized that he was at the strange house in the English countryside.

A few seconds later, as if to remind himself further, he let out a burp from one end of his body and a fart from the other, and he reflected upon the fact that even after a decent nap he still felt absolutely stuffed full of food.

Swinging his legs over the side of the bed, he got to his feet. He took a few steps toward the door, before stopping as he saw some scratches on the wall. Making his way closer, he realized that these scratches were similar to the ones George had shown him in another bedroom; he knew that most likely there was a perfectly reasonable explanation, yet as he ran a hand across the scratches and traced their lengths he was unable to shake the feeling that perhaps some madman had once been trying desperately to claw his way out of the place.

"The English are a strange breed," he muttered, turning and traipsing out onto the landing, holding his hands out so as to make sure that he didn't walk straight into a wall. The darkness was becoming all-encompassing now and he wasn't even sure that he could find the stairs without risking falling down. "The strangest in the world, I'd mark."

As he placed a hand on the banister, he heard it creak loudly. He gave it a little wiggle and noted that the entire house seemed to have been left to fall apart, which seemed stranger given that – despite its rather remote location – the place seemed fairly decent. Then again, there was certainly a strange atmosphere and a few seconds later that fact was underlined as he heard a series of creaks and groans coming from somewhere high above.

Looking up, he saw a thick rafter running across the ceiling above the stairs. For a moment he swore he could hear a rope straining and swinging, although the sensation passed after a second and he quickly dismissed it as nothing more than a product of his imagination.

He burped again, and then he noticed that the house was exceedingly quiet. Silent, even. And despite the supposed presence of a housekeeper, there seemed to be no light or warmth downstairs.

"Hello?" he called out. "Mrs. Baxter?"

He waited.

Silence.

"George, are you back yet?"

Again, he heard no reply.

"What can be taking so long?" he muttered as he began to make his way down the stairs, stepping loudly since he had no care to conceal his presence. "I thought housekeepers were supposed to provide a certain degree of comfort, yet this place is as cold as the grave itself."

Reaching the bottom of the stairs, he looked around. There was still no sign of anyone, but he was sick of the darkness so he stepped into the old study and began to examine some candles that had been left in ornamental candlesticks on a shelf. Picking one up, he reasoned that there would be no harm in lighting a few, so he turned to go and find a flame he could use. And then as he stepped into the hallway once more, he heard a brief but very clear interrupted cry.

He stood completely still, and although the cry was gone now, he felt sure that he had heard a voice – a man, indeed – call out for help.

"Hello?" he said again, more cautiously this time. "George, is that you? Are you back?"

He walked over to the door opposite and looked into one of the rooms, but in truth the scene was too dark for him to really see much at all.

"George," he continued, "you're not injured, are you? I'm just trying to find a way to light this candle, I know you said that we shouldn't show any brightness at night in case we draw attention to our presence here, but I'm quite sure that we're far enough away from civilization. Nobody from the village is going to notice one single candle, are they?"

Silence.

"George?"

Unable to shake a sense of unease, he waited for a moment before turning to go back out across the hallway. At the last moment, however, he let out a shocked gasp as he spotted a darkened figure standing just a few feet away.

"Mr. Vowles?" a woman's voice asked. "I had thought you might sleep all through the night and into tomorrow morning."

"Mrs. Baxter," he stammered, unable to hide the fact that he was a little startled by her sudden return, "there you are. I'm sorry, I was starting to think that you must have left for the day."

"Left?" She paused, her face still shrouded

in darkness. "Oh, I think you misunderstand, Mr. Vowles. I don't ever leave. This is my home."

"You... live here?"

"I suppose you might say that," she said calmly. "Perhaps. But the point is, I am always here."

She stepped forward, and then she reached out in the darkness and took the candle from his hands.

"You must be in search of a little light," she suggested. "I'm so dreadfully sorry, Sir, I should have had all of that waiting for you upon your return from slumber. I allowed myself to become distracted, but it will not happen again."

"That's quite alright," he told her, and he liked the fact that she was so clearly showing him some respect. "This time."

"Allow me to set you at ease," she continued. "Would you like to sit down and perhaps enjoy a mug of ale?"

"Ale?" He considered the possibility for a moment; he wasn't a heavy drinker, that much was certain, but in that particular instant the idea of a quick libation actually appealed. "Well, I suppose it would be rude of me to turn down such a kind offer," he admitted, "although I did not know that you had any ale here at the house."

"Oh, we have almost anything you could possibly want," she told him. "Please, come through to the study."

"Would it be possible to light a fire?" he asked as he fumbled his way across the dark hallway.

"A fire, Sir?"

"Just a small one. George doesn't want us to give away our location, but I feel certain that nobody is watching us that closely."

"This way, Sir," she said, walking ahead of him into the study and approaching the hearth. "I find that this room is particularly suited to the task of evening contemplation, and you'll see that the fire in the hearth still lingers."

"It does?"

As he stepped closer, he saw her kneeling in front of the fireplace. He was about to tell here that there had clearly been no fire in that fireplace for quite some time, but at the last second he realized that he could just about see the faintest red glow. He had no idea how he'd missed the fact that there was even *some* heat coming from the fireplace, and he had to admit that Mrs. Baxter certainly seemed to have a few tricks up her sleeves. She was a miracle, and she seemed almost too good to be true.

"A man could get used to this," he murmured.

"What was that, Sir?"

"Nothing," he added abruptly, aware that he had to remain strong. After all, he had a mission to complete. "My associate Mr. Jones should be back by now. Is there any sign of him?"

"I don't see him anywhere," she replied, as she carefully lit the candle and then placed it on the side, bringing a flickering glow to the room. After that, she slowly got to her feet. "Do you?"

"I suppose he's still out there," he muttered, looking at the boxes in the corner. "He suggested that we shouldn't have any light out here at night, in case we attract attention. As much as I like the candle, I wonder whether -"

"I don't think one candle is going to cause any harm, is it?" Fanny purred. "It's just to bring some heat and comfort to you, Sir. I'm sure you need that. You certainly deserve the chance to rest."

"I suppose I do."

"And I have some more food for you."

"I'm really rather full."

"Nonsense," she replied, stepping past him, brushing against him in the process. "Wait here for just a moment and then I shall have a bedtime snack prepared. You're a big, strong man and I imagine you have some hard work ahead of you tomorrow."

"I believe we shall be finishing our preparations for -"

He caught himself just in time.

"Well," he added carefully, "for other matters."

"I'm sure," she said as she left the room.

"It's my job to look after you, and I'm going to do just that. Please, Mr. Vowles, warm yourself for a few minutes until the food is ready."

"I suppose it can't hurt," he replied, stepping over to the fireplace and holding his hands out. To his surprise, he *did* feel a faint flicker of warmth, and he told himself that the light from the candle was really not strong enough to raise an alarm from the village. "Everyone else gets some light and heat. Why shouldn't *I*?"

As he continued to heat his hands, he heard the sound of wind battering the house, causing some of the wooden boards to shake. At least, that's what he thought he heard, even if he failed to notice that most of the noise was coming from somewhere beneath his feet.

CHAPTER THIRTEEN

THE FOLLOWING MORNING, A cold wind whipped through the cemetery as a small group stood gathered around an open grave.

"We ask for your mercy, Lord," Father Brown said as the coffin was lowered into the ground, "as this soul is sent to you for judgment."

Patience felt a shudder run through her chest. She kept her eyes fixed on the coffin, and she couldn't help thinking of her father's aged face. Earlier she had seen him one last time, before the coffin was nailed shut, and she had been struck by the lack of peace; whereas usually dead bodies showed some degree of rest, her father's corpse had looked plagued by the ills and evils of the world, as if even in death he had not been able to escape from the horrors of Hadlow House.

As if, she thought now, Fanny Baxter was still somehow reaching out to torment his soul.

"It's done," Daniel murmured, turning to her, and she realized that she hadn't been listening to everything the priest had said. She glanced around, feeling somewhat bemused, and then she turned to Father Brown and saw a kind smile on his face.

"Oh," she stammered, trying to seem at least somewhat present, "thank you. Thank you everyone. You have all been most kind."

"Would you like to go home now?" Daniel asked her.

"I think I would like a moment of reflection," she told him, as she looked at the grave again. "Just to... remind myself."

"Of course." He touched the side of her arm. "I shall go to the gate and speak with Father Brown, and you can take as much time as you need."

"Thank you," she said softly, although she felt rather uneasy as he and the others walked away from the grave. "Thank you, all of you. You've been most generous with your time."

Once she was alone, Patience realized that this was the moment she had been dreading. She knew not what to say to her father's coffin, and in truth she had been unable to properly settle her thoughts ever since he had first stumbled back into the village. The coffin looked so austere and bare down at the bottom of the grave, and Patience couldn't help but worry that her father's soul was most likely far from rest. She wanted to pray for him, to ask the Lord to forgive his many transgressions, but at the same time she couldn't help remembering the sensation of the knife's blade twisting in her belly.

And then, a moment later, she realized that she could hear a scratching sound.

Turning and looking across the cemetery, she expected to see some simple explanation, but instead there was no sign of anyone. She saw only the assorted gravestones, yet at the same time this scratching noise became stronger and more persistent, almost as if someone or something was trying to catch her attention. She waited for a few more seconds, and then – drawn by an innate sense of curiosity – she stepped past her father's freshly-dug grave and set out to find the source of the sound. Even as she picked her way between the graves, however, she felt a tingling sensation in the back of her mind as if deep down she already knew exactly what and who was drawing her closer.

She almost tripped on the uneven ground, but finally she spotted a particular grave up ahead. And as she reached that grave, she felt a shudder run through her body as she read the name.

"Frances Baxter," she whispered.

As soon as those words left her lips, the

scratching sound intensified. Reaching up, she touched the right side of her head, and she worried for a moment that some type of insect might have burrowed its way into her ear. She briefly imagined its thin little legs scratching at the inside of her ear canal, but after a few seconds she lowered her hand again as she realize that this sound was most certainly coming from elsewhere.

The sound was coming from the grave.

Looking down at the uneven grass, she thought of Frances Baxter's coffin down there in the depths, and somehow she knew that the scratching sound was coming from beneath that coffin's lid.

In her mind's eye, she now saw Fanny flat on her back in the darkness, furiously digging at the wood. She knew of course that Fanny had been dead for many years; the gravestone noted 1689 as the year of her passing, which meant that she had been gone now for some eighty-six years. Indeed, even if the woman had somehow not died, she would be almost one hundred and fifty years old, which was simply impossible. As she continued to stare at the grave, therefore, and as the scratching sound persisted, Patience knew full well that the woman was most surely long dead, but that somehow her spirit had lingered.

And now, evidently, her body persisted too.

Although Daniel had warned her to not let her thoughts dwell on such matters, now Patience couldn't help wondering about some connection between the body in the ground and the spirit in the house. Was it possible, she pondered, that in some manner Fanny was reaching out from her grave and inhabiting the house in that manner? In which case, was it not logical to assume that destroying her earthly remains might in some way end her reign of terror? Patience knew that the idea was extreme, and that nobody would countenance the digging up of a woman's body from hallowed ground, let alone the possibility of then destroying that body. Then again, was it not the case that nobody else – nobody apart from Patience – understood the full horror of Fanny's vengeance?

"Why can't you just rest?" she whispered now. "What happened to you in your life to leave you like this? Why are you so evil? Were you not once a good woman? What changed and made you -"

Suddenly the scratching sound twisted in her ear, bringing a brief flicker of pain.

"Can you hear me?" she asked through gritted teeth. "What did I ever do to make you hate me so much? What did my family do? We merely moved into that house and tried to live honest, happy lives. Why did you take it upon yourself to punish us like this?"

The scratching became faster and more furious, and now Patience felt she could hear another sound mixed in with the first; she told herself that she might very well be mistaken, but she furrowed her brow as she realized that she could hear wood cracking, almost as if Fanny was slowly but surely making her way through the coffin's lid.

And then what?

Would she eventually dig her way out of the grave entirely? Until her father's death, Patience had told herself that the ghost of Fanny Baxter was mercifully contained within the walls of Hadlow House, but now she began to contemplate the impossible: what if, after so many years, Fanny had discovered some new way of escaping from those shackles and -

"Patience?"

Startled, she turned to find Daniel standing directly behind her. From the concern on his face, she immediately realized that he was troubled, and she found herself wondering just how long she had spent standing at Fanny Baxter's grave. She turned to look down at the stone, poised to ask her husband whether he too heard the scratching sound, but in that moment she realized that silence had returned.

"Patience, are you alright?" Daniel asked. "There are a few people waiting at *The Shoemaker*, but we are under no obligation to -"

"No, we must be polite," she replied, before swallowing hard. "To be honest, I would be glad of the distraction, for I confess that my mind is troubled."

"You're thinking about events up at the house again," he observed as he looked down at the grave. "I understand why, but I pray that you start to see things a little differently. That house is empty now and it can harm no-one."

"I know."

"And it shall remain that way," he added. "Forever, if I get my way, but most certainly for the remainder of our lives. We cannot determine what will happen to the place two hundred years hence, or three or four hundred years, although I hope that by such a point it will have rotten away to nothing." He paused, watching her eyes and studying her reaction, and finally he tapped her tenderly on the nose before taking her by the hand. "Let us go and try to be our usual selves," he added. "Now that your father has been properly buried, we might yet be able to put such troubled thoughts from our minds."

"I hope so," she told him as they walked away. "Truly, I do."

Behind them, the uneven grass lay six feet above the battered coffin that still contained – after all these years, shrouded in darkness – the skeletal remains of Fanny Baxter.

CHAPTER FOURTEEN

"I AM STUFFED TO the gills," Thomas Vowles said, waddling slightly as he made his way across the hallway of Hadlow House. Rubbing his belly, he let out another burp. "I did not think I would be able to fit in much breakfast, Mrs. Baxter, but you insisted that I should try and perhaps you had a point."

Reaching the door to the study, he looked through and saw her sitting at the table. Furrowing his brow, he realized that she was running a single fingertip against the table's top, digging her nail deep enough to cause a faint scratching sound.

"Mrs. Baxter?" he said cautiously, as late morning light shone through the window. "I think I must go and try to find George today. It is most unlike him to be absent overnight."

"What did you say?" she asked airily, before turning to him. "Who is George?"

"Jones," he replied. "George Jones, my... associate."

"Oh, of course." She hesitated, as if she was still lost in thought, and then she got to her feet. "I really wouldn't worry, Mr. Vowles. I'm sure he's quite alright. He seemed capable of taking care of himself."

"You saw him, then? I had believed that you only arrived after he left yesterday."

"I spied him briefly. Did you enjoy your breakfast?"

"I did," he exclaimed with a satisfied smile, "although I confess that I have never before seen so much meat on one plate, or such a variety! I am actually sweating from it a little."

"You're a busy man," she said, stepping past him, brushing against his shoulder once more in a manner that he'd noticed was becoming more common. "I've told you before, you need to maintain your strength."

"I have not been so well taken care of since I was a little boy," he observed.

"You need to be ready for your next exploits," she said, before stopping at the door that led into the kitchen. Not turning to him, she hesitated for a few seconds. "You and your associate have placed several boxes in the study. I can't help but wonder what is in them."

"That's a private matter," he said awkwardly.

"As the housekeeper here, I should like to know," she told him. "I might have duties to perform with them."

"I'd rather keep that whole situation private," he replied. "Between George and myself. I trust that you understand."

"Do you have any thing to hide?" she asked, still not turning to him.

"Hide?" he replied, and now he reached up and adjusted his collar as if he felt increasingly uncomfortable. "Absolutely not. Why would you ask such a thing? Are people talking in the village?"

"I would hardly know what is being said in the village," she told him coldly.

"Mr. Jones and I are merely visiting England for a while," Thomas went on. "There's really nothing more to it than that, and no need for suspicion. Despite the current situation and the machinations of the government, we are certainly great fans of His Royal Highness King George."

"King George?"

Seemingly struck by that name, she half-turned to him.

"Of course," she added, "the years go by and the world continues to change. I should not expect anything else and I am sure this King George is a good and noble ruler."

"There are some who might disagree on a few points," Thomas replied, before patting his belly again, "but as for me, I really should see where *my* George has gone. As I've said, he's a very careful and ordered man and I really don't think that he would ever wander off in such a manner. He's also not liable to get himself into trouble, so I'm quite sure he has the situation in hand, but I'd like to know for certain." He turned and began to lumber toward the front door. "I shan't be too long, though. I'm sure there's absolutely no cause for concern."

"Indeed," she whispered as she heard him walking out of the house. She hesitated, before turning to look at the dining room door as she heard the faintest sobbing sound. "Not now," she snarled. "I'm sick of your pathetic blathering. Don't make me punish you."

She waited, and the sound quickly stopped.

"That's better," she murmured, before turning and walking to the door that led to the space under the stairs and swiftly disappearing from sight.

***

"Help me!" George gasped, pulling once again on the bottom step as he tried in vain to drag himself up the wooden staircase. "Please, somebody just -"

Stopping suddenly, he looked up into the

darkness and realized that he could hear the sound of footsteps descending. He froze for a moment, terrified, and then he pulled back into the corner. Pressing himself against the cold, slightly damp stones of the wall, he listened as the footsteps made their way closer, but deep down he already knew exactly what was happening.

"Please," he stammered, barely able to get any words out at all, "don't -"

"Must everyone whimper in this infernal manner?" Fanny asked, her voice sounding a little scratchy in the pitch darkness. "You are trying my patience."

"Thomas!" he tried to shout, although he could only manage to raise his voice to a faint cry. "Where in damnation are you, man? I'm down here! Why can't you hear me!"

"Your associate is rather distracted at present," Fanny said calmly, "and besides, he has left the house for a short while."

"Damn you," George said breathlessly. "What kind of foul demon are you?"

"You speak with much venom," she replied, "for one who has lost so much blood. But tell me, what is in those containers that your associate brought into the house?"

"That's none of your business!"

"I am the housekeeper," she pointed out, "so everything that enters this place is my concern. You had him carry in several boxes, but I am afraid that I have not been able to ascertain their contents. You will tell me now, or I shall tear more strips from your body and feed them to your miserable pig of a friend."

"You won't stop us," he groaned.

"Stop what, exactly?"

"There are others like us," he continued. "Others who will fight for what is right. This parliament of England has grown rotten and unfit for its very purpose, and your king shows signs of madness. Already there are whispers in the streets that he has to be helped with the most basic of tasks. The colonies must be freed from the insanity of King George's reign. It is a maladie that will only get worse."

"Do you think I care about such things?" she asked. "I care only about this house and what is in it. Tell me about the boxes."

"Why? So you can interfere?"

"You are a most tiresome fellow," she muttered. "I thought Mr. Hadlow was obstinate, but you are another breed entirely. What is it going to take, I wonder, for you to come to your senses? I'm not even sure that there is much point in keeping you here, not when you are so evidently unwilling to compromise."

She paused, and after a few seconds the door at the top of the wooden steps began to creak open, allowing a sliver of light through into the passage that led down into the house's basement. Now, at last, George was able to see the silhouette of his tormentor and – as his eyes adjusted a little more – the fierce anger in her eyes.

"Madame, what are you?" he sneered. "Nothing godly, I can tell."

"You are insignificant," she replied, "and not worthy of the slightest, briefest thought. Indeed, you have become an irritant of the highest order. The only value you have seemed to possess is that you can be used to sustain your friend up there, but I am starting to think that there is one other thing you can do for me."

"I would never do anything for you!" he snapped angrily. "I would rather die!"

"Oh, you *will* die," she told him, before holding up an ornate candlestick that she had brought from upstairs, "but it is in the manner of that death that you shall be of the greatest benefit."

"I would rather burn in the depths of Hell," he replied as she stepped closer, "than help you and -"

Suddenly she leaned down and plunged the candlestick's sharp tip into his shoulder, twisting it as she forced it deeper and deeper. And as George cried out in absolute agony, Fanny's only response was dig the candlestick even harder into his shoulder until finally its bloodied tip broke out through the back of his shoulder.

CHAPTER FIFTEEN

"BUT HOW CAN YOU be sure?" Patience asked as she stood in the main room at the front of *The Shoemaker*, having somewhat cornered Father Brown near the bar. "Just because the bodies are buried in sacred ground, that doesn't mean they're necessarily at peace."

"You must rest assured that all is well," the priest told her, while glancing around in the hope that he might find someone who could rescue him. "Perhaps your husband would be better at explaining this all to you, I'm sure that he must be around here somewhere in the -"

"Have you ever heard a scratching sound out there?"

"I beg your -"

"As if somebody is trying to claw their way

out of a coffin," Patience continued. "You have an imagination, so try to use it and imagine what that would sound like. Imagine someone using their fingertips – perhaps with no skin or nail, just bone – to try to dig their way out from their own grave."

"Are you talking about the accidental burial of the dead?" he asked. "If so -"

"I'm not talking about that at all," she said firmly, interrupting him yet again. In fact, she had barely let him complete so much as a single sentence since she'd caught up to him. "I'm talking about the souls of the dead!"

As Father Brown signed and tried to calm Patience's nerves, Anne slipped through the crowd of adults and tried to work out what she could do next. She hadn't been allowed to go to the cemetery; all she'd been told was that her great-grandfather had died recently and was being buried, and she didn't really mind that she wasn't going to be able to see his coffin lowered into the ground. After all, she hadn't ever met the man, and she hadn't even known that he was still alive until suddenly everyone had started talking about him being dead. Now, however, she found herself surrounded by adults who were all talking about very dull things, and she had to admit that she was bored.

"I just want to play," she said, looking down at the tattered rag-doll in her right hand. "Is that too much to ask for?"

The rag-doll stared back at her with its smiling face, but this really wasn't much help.

Stepping out through to the rear of the building, Anne finally emerged in small hallway that led into the courtyard. There were more adults out there, and she could already tell that they were talking about much the same things as the adults inside, so she turned and instead saw a set of stairs leading up toward the inn's higher floor. She knew she probably wasn't supposed to explore, but at the same time she found herself wondering what the upstairs of an inn actually looked like, so after a moment she began to pick her way up the staircase, following its winding course until she reached the top and found herself on a fairly nondescript landing.

Looking around, she realized that this really wasn't much more interesting than the rest of the building. She briefly considered exploring the rooms, before turning to head back down. And then she stopped as she saw that a length of rope had fallen down from one of the rafters above and was dangling in front of her face.

"How -"

She felt sure that this rope hadn't been there before. Reaching out, she touched its looped end and found that it had been left tied in a peculiar manner. This made little sense to her, of course, and she couldn't help but wonder who would ever need such a thing in a public house. Then again, she had no real idea what people got up to in a place such as *The Shoemaker*, so after a moment she simply tugged on the rope and found that it was held pretty firmly in place. She looked up at the rafters again, before stepping past the rope and starting to go back downstairs.

As she reached the halfway point, however, she stopped and looked down at her right hand. The rag-doll was gone; she didn't remember losing it anywhere, but when she turned around she saw that it was on the landing. Reasoning that she must have dropped it without noticing, she hurried back up the stairs and grabbed the doll.

"Silly thing," she said with a faint smile, before turning and almost running back to the top of the staircase. "You're really not very clever, are you? What do you think's going to happen if you fall onto the floor and I can't -"

Suddenly her left foot slipped on the top step. Startled, she reached out to support herself but her hands missed the railing and she fell forward. Before she had a chance to react, her head slipped into the rope's loop and she let out a gasp as she felt the noose tighten around her neck. She struggling immediately to get free, but this only caused the rope to tighten even more as her feet fell forward and she found herself hanging in the stairwell.

"Help!" she gasped, even though she could

barely get her voice about a strangled whisper. "Grandma! Grandpa! Help me!"

As she continued to try to break free, the rag-doll fell from the hand and tumbled own the stairs, landing in a crumpled heap at the bottom.

***

"I really think that you need to take this onboard properly," Father Brown said firmly, still stuck talking to Patience in the inn's front room. "The bodies in our cemetery are at rest, Mrs. Purkiss. They have been accepted into the care of the Lord, and of the church, and now their earthly struggles are over."

"But what if they don't *want* their earthly struggles to be over?" she asked increasingly keenly, as if she was struggling to stay calm. "What if they're pushing and pushing to come back and get revenge?"

"Such things are simply not possible," he told her, before spotting a familiar figure nearby. "Ah, Mr. Purkiss!" he called out. "I have been talking to your wife!"

"Have you seen Anne?" Daniel asked as he made his way over. He glanced around for a moment. "I haven't laid eyes on the girl almost since we got here."

"You don't know everything about the

dead!" Patience told Father Brown. "I've seen things that you can't even imagine!"

"Mr. Purkiss," Father Brown said with a sigh, "perhaps -"

"I've seen the dead walk!" she continued. "Out at Hadlow House, I saw Frances Baxter and I think I saw some other ghosts as well! If you don't believe me, ask Daniel!"

"There was an... incident many years ago," Daniel said cautiously, clearly worried that he might be taken for a fool. "More than fifty years ago, actually." He hesitated. "But that is in the past and -"

"One of your predecessors died out there!" Patience snapped angrily, grabbing Father Brown's arm. "Father Ward was killed by that spirit!"

"I have heard about poor Father Ward," Father Brown replied cautiously, "and it is my understanding that the circumstances surrounding his unfortunate demise were never satisfactorily explained. Nevertheless, I would caution against using inflammatory language when we actually don't know whether -"

"He died because she killed him!" Patience hissed. "She snapped his neck or... she did something horribly cruel to end his life! He was a man of the cloth, a man of God, and she murdered him in that house! Doesn't that tell you something about the evil that festers in her heart? And now that same woman's corpse is buried in the cemetery at St. Leonard's, and everyone seems to think that just because it's holy ground she's going to be contained forever, but I'm absolutely certain that she's getting stronger and stronger! Soon no-one will be safe!"

She waited for a response, but in that moment she realized that the entire inn had fallen silent. Everyone was staring at her, and she understood now that in her state of panic and agitation she must have raised her voice so that she could be heard even on the other side of the room. She opened her mouth to tell them that everything she'd just claimed was true, but now she realized that so many of the faces staring back at her with filled with expressions of pure pity. How, she wondered, could she ever make them understand that the ghost of Fanny Baxter was dangerous?

Suddenly a scream rang out, coming from the hallway. Turning, Patience looked toward the open door that led to the back of the building, and a fraction of a second later the barmaid stumbled back into view with the most anguished sense of pure horror on her face.

"Help!" she shouted. "It's the young girl! Somebody has to help her!"

CHAPTER SIXTEEN

"GEORGE! ARE YOU OUT here? George, where in all damnation are you?"

Stumbling a little as he made his way down a steep muddy verge, Thomas Vowles finally stopped for a moment as he found himself at the edge of a winding country road. He hadn't expected to emerge from the forest at the edge of civilization, but in truth he'd become more than a little lost and he was glad of the chance to get his bearings. Indeed, as he looked around, he spotted the spire of Cobblefield's church in the distance beyond some trees, and he realized that he must be on the very same road that he and George had taken on their way out to Hadlow House.

Still slightly out of breath, he looked both ways along the road as he tried to work out what to do next. He didn't want to worry, of course, and he knew that George was more than capable of looking after himself, yet...

Yet he couldn't help but wonder whether something might be wrong.

"You'll be back," he muttered under his breath, before turning and making his way along the road. "If I'm not very much -"

Stopping suddenly, he saw a figure walking toward him. He froze, wondering briefly whether this might be George, before realizing that it was in fact an elderly man leaning on a stick. For a few seconds Thomas considered ducking out of sight into the bushes lining the road, but he supposed that he was too late and – besides – some random old man didn't seem to pose much of a threat. He might even, Thomas realized after a moment, be of some use.

"Hello there, Sir!" he called out as the man made his way closer. "This is a fine day for a walk!"

"It's that, certainly," the man replied, visibly in a little pain as he leaned harder and harder on the stick. He stopped a few paces away and looked Thomas up and down. "I haven't seen you in these parts before."

"I am merely passing through," Thomas told him, and now it was his turn make an inspection as he spotted some heavy-looking bags hanging from the man's belt. "Are you a trader?"

"I'm a little of one thing," the man replied with a faint smile, "and a little of several others."

He paused, watching Thomas with what seemed to be a growing sense of suspicion.

"Are you lost, Sir?" he continued.

"I'm not lost," Thomas replied, which he reasoned was true enough. "Are *you* lost?"

"I live not half an hour's walk from this very spot," the man told him. "If I were lost here, I think I might be losing my mind."

"Fair enough," Thomas muttered, still eyeing the man's bags and wondering whether they might contain gold or something else of value. "I suppose there's no harm in two people meeting out on the road, is there?"

"Not as far as I can see," the man said, before starting to shuffle forward. "I bid you good day, Sir, and perhaps I'll see you again."

"Yes, perhaps," Thomas replied, watching carefully as the man made his way past. A moment later he spotted a small rock resting at the side of the road.

"I don't meet many people out here," the man continued, wincing once again as he limped and leaned on his stick. "Not that I mind, of course. I have no problem making pleasant conversation with anyone I meet. It's just that this particular road tends not to be very busy, Sir, on account of it not leading directly to anywhere. There are quicker routes to some of the other villages, although some still prefer to come this way, but out here there's only -"

Stopping suddenly, he stared down at the road's rough surface.

"Oh, but there's one thing you should be aware of," he murmured. "Yes, that's very important. If you don't know the area, you might not know about the house. It's probably nothing, just a load of superstition, but I always find it's best to keep out of trouble." He began to turn to Thomas. "There's a house in the woods, Sir, that's best left -"

Before he could finish, Thomas brought the rock crashing down against the side of his head. Not even having time to let out a cry, the man crumpled to the ground, letting his stick fall away at the side. He immediately tried to get up, but Thomas brought the rock smashing into the top of his head, cracking his skull and killing him instantly. As the man slumped down dead, blood splattered against the road, and already Thomas was crouching down and pulling the bags away from the man's belt.

"What do we have here?" he muttered excitedly. "I could use some luck, preferably a little gold or -"

In that moment, several pebbles fell from the bags and landed in the palm of his hand. He checked the other bags, and then he threw the last of the pebbles aside as he sighed and got to his feet.

"What kind of infernal fool walks around carrying a collection of such things?" he snapped angrily, before kicking the dead man hard in the shoulder. "Are you simple in the head? Why would you fill up tiny sacks with small rocks? Don't you realize that you're liable to give the wrong impression?" He looked down at the dead man's face, before kicking him again. "What a complete waste of your time *and* mine," he added, before grabbing the man's wrists and dragging him off the road. "I really don't have time for this, you know. I'm on an important mission and -"

Out of breath once more, he dropped the man behind a large bush and then took a moment to wipe his hands.

"Not that I should tell you," he said, rolling his eyes. "I might not believe in ghosts or anything foolish like that, but one still shouldn't tempt fate. Thanks for absolutely nothing, you stupid old idiot. I hope you realize that you brought this whole situation upon yourself."

With that he turned and walked away. In the process, he inadvertently kicked several of the rocks that the old man had collected, scattering them across the road as he headed off toward the turning that led to Hadlow House.

***

"Help me!" George gasped, reaching forward and grabbing the root of a tree, then tensing for a moment before pulling himself forward a few more precious inches. "Somebody..."

Barely able to raise his voice above a pained gasp, he stopped and looked around. Ever since he'd dragged his ailing body out of Hadlow House, somehow escaping from the dreadful woman who'd captured him, he'd been trying to find safety. He'd taken to hauling himself across the forest floor using his one good arm; the other arm had long since become too numb to use, thanks mainly to the candlestick that remained lodged in his shoulder. Having tried to remove the candlestick at one point, he'd found that any movement at all caused much blood to gush from the wound, so he'd left it in place for now while he desperately tried to reach safety.

"Help me," he whimpered, even though he knew most likely there was nobody nearby to hear him. He hadn't even managed to keep track of which way he'd gone after leaving the house. "Please..."

Somehow he'd managed to drag himself up the stairs and into the hallway of Hadlow House, and then over to the front door, which had mercifully been left open. He had no idea how he'd been able to escape, and he'd expected the horrific woman to grab him at any moment, but he could only reason that she must have been suddenly distracted as he'd made his bid for freedom. In the time she'd kept him as a prisoner in the basement, she'd cut off several large chunks of meat and muscle from his body, and this had left him feeling terribly weak, but the need to survive kept him going.

He knew, however, that he would die soon if he couldn't find help.

Taking hold of another root, he braced himself for the pain that would inevitably follow. He clenched his teeth, and then he hauled himself past the root, only to find that he was at the top of a gentle slope. He hesitated, wondering whether he should turn back, but he realized after a few seconds that there appeared to be a road at the slope's bottom. Unable to help himself, he leaned forward and rolled down, letting out a series of pained gasps as his battered and bloodied body hit several thick obstacles on the way, until finally he rolled out onto the road and came to a stop with one final gasp.

Once he'd managed to summon a little more strength, he looked both ways along the road. The stretch seemed vaguely familiar, as if perhaps it was the route from the village to that infernal house, and after a few seconds he spotted the spire of a church. Realizing that this must be the way to Cobblefield, he briefly considered trying to get help in the village, but he knew there would be too many questions. His best bet, he supposed, was to find some way to get far away from the area, and he told himself that he could probably just about ride a horse. In that case, he decided that his best option was to get back around to the front of the house and try to get onto the horse without attracting any attention.

That way, he might also be able to find Thomas.

He turned to crawl along the road, knocking some small pebbles aside in the process, only to stop as he saw a man riding a horse in his direction. Already his mind was racing as he realized that – in his beaten state – he was going to have to come up with a convincing story to explain what had happened without arousing suspicion.

"What do we have here?" the man on horseback asked as he brought his steed to a halt just a few paces away. "Sir, are you in need of assistance?" He glanced around for a moment, before looking down at George again. "I'm searching for my father, he has escaped from a local lunatic asylum. But you, I perceive, would seem to be in a rather bad way."

CHAPTER SEVENTEEN

"GRANDMOTHER, I'M FINE!" ANNE protested, trying again to sit up in bed. "I only -"

"You're not fine!" Patience hissed, pushing her back down. "Do you have any idea how close you came to death?"

"I just fell!"

"What was that rope even doing there?"

"John says he has no idea," Daniel reminded her from the doorway. "He thinks he might have used it to hang pheasants last year, but he can't be sure. The point is -"

"The point is, another thirty seconds and there would have been no hope," Patience replied, as she began to frantically check the marks around Anne's throat. "My darling, are you quite sure you were alone up there? Think carefully, are you certain that you didn't see or hear a woman who might have hurt you?"

"There was no-one else there," Anne replied, and she was close to tears now as she turned to Daniel. "Grandpa, can't you tell her to stop worrying? I just had an accident, that's all. I'm sorry, I won't let it happen again."

"I think she could use some rest," Daniel suggested.

"I'm not letting you out of my sight!" Patience told Anne. "Do you understand? I know you think you're too old for me to fuss, but you're simply wrong about that! You're only eleven years old, and your mother wanted me to keep you safe. If you feel that I'm being over-protective, then I'm afraid that there's nothing we can do about that fact. You're simply going to have to accept that you're just a child."

"This is getting us nowhere," Daniel observed. "Patience, I really think that Anne needs to sleep, and we have to accept that she simply had a very unfortunate accident. There is no more to it."

"Grandpa's right," Anne said softly. "Grandma, please, there was no-one else there and it was just a fall. You don't have to be so horrible and -"

Suddenly Patience slapped her hard on the side of the face, causing the girl to pull back in shock.

"Don't speak to me like that when I'm only trying to keep you safe!" Patience snapped angrily, before getting to her feet and storming out of the room. "You have no idea what's out there, Anne. You're just a stupid little girl and you don't realize that we might all be in danger!"

"I'm sorry!" Anne sobbed as tears streamed down her face. "Grandma, why are you so upset at me?"

"Try to get some rest," Daniel told her. "I'm sure everything will be alright in the morning."

***

Standing in the bedroom with the front of her dress open, Patience stared into the mirror as she ran a hand over the scars on her belly.

"You didn't need to strike the girl," Daniel said, stopping in the doorway.

"I had to get some sense into her somehow."

"Not like that," he replied. "You've never struck her before, Patience. I fear that you're letting this whole situation take over your -"

"If you have nothing useful to say, then you might as well leave me alone," she replied, still examining the scar. She paused for a moment as her fingertips ran across the knotted lines of twisted skin. "I know what you're thinking," she added. "You're thinking that I'm being far too protective, especially considering that Anne isn't even my..."

Her voice trailed off for a few seconds.

"My flesh and blood," she added as tears reached her eyes.

"Patience -"

"It's true," she added, interrupting him. "I always wanted children of my own, but after my father did this to me, I was unable to carry any. And then your dear sister died during childbirth, as many of the women in your family have done, and we raised her daughter as our own. Then she too died in the same way, and we raised *her* daughter as our granddaughter. She is your flesh and blood, Daniel, but she is not mine. That doesn't mean, however, that I don't feel as if I have to protect her."

"You have done more for that girl, and for her mother, than any real -"

He stopped himself just in time.

"You know what I mean," he continued, stepping over to her and putting his hands on her shoulders from behind. He kissed the side of her face, and then he looked at her reflection in the mirror as she continued to examine her scar. "Those girls are so lucky to have had you in their lives, and while you might not be of the same blood, you have been a mother and a grandmother to them."

"If she knew -"

"She will never find out."

"But if we were honest and told her that I

am not really her grandmother, how do you think she would react?"

"She would understand," he replied, "because she is a kind and intelligent girl, but there is really no need to worry about any of this. What happened to Anne today was an accident. No more and no less."

"You don't know that," she said darkly. "Her head was in that noose, Daniel. It was exactly like the fate that my own mother met."

"Patience -"

"It was Fanny!" she snapped, turning to him. "You have to know it in your heart, Daniel! She has been contained in that house for so long but I fear she is breaking out and reaching toward us!" She sighed. "I should have made us move away a long time ago, but I thought it better to stay near the house so that I could keep everyone away from it. Now I think we should simply leave Cobblefield behind forever and let other people take their own risks. I will not sacrifice our family's safety for the sake of these people!"

"We've talked about this before," he told her. "We *can't* leave, I would have no livelihood anywhere else."

"You could find something!"

"It's not as easy as that," he pointed out. "Patience, I know that Anne's accident carries painful echoes of what happened to your mother all those years ago, but you mustn't let this coincidence drive you out of your mind. I said that Anne needed to rest, and I believe that you do as well. Can you please try to calm your racing thoughts?"

"What if -"

"This was not Fanny's work," he said firmly. "Her ghost is still at Hadlow House, where it has always been, and where it will remain. Your father escaped, and evidently she was not able to drag him back, so that should prove the point further." He watched her tear-filled eyes, waiting for a response. "So long as we don't set foot in that place," he added, "we are safe from her. Forever."

"You can't be sure of that."

"I can." He leaned forward and kissed her on the forehead. "The afternoon is drawing on," he continued, "and I must go and deal with a few matters across the village. Can I trust you, Patience, to stay here and to turn your mind to other matters?"

"I shall try," she told him, although she sounded far from confident.

"I'll be back soon," he said, turning and heading to the doorway before stopping and looking back at her. "That night you escaped from Hadlow House," he added, "was the night Fanny Baxter lost her ability to hurt you. Your father was already a broken man by that point, he carried that damage with him and that's why he stabbed you. But Fanny herself is forever trapped in that place and there's absolutely nothing she can do to hurt any of us, not unless we ever set foot in that house again. Which we're hardly likely to do."

"I hope you're right," she told him. "I pray that you are."

"I am, and now I shall go out so that I can be back before darkness. Try to rest, Patience, or keep your mind busy. One or the other."

"I'll do my best," she said softly as she was left alone. Taking a deep breath, she listened to the sound of her husband leaving the house, and then she turned to go through to the pantry. "I only hope that I am strong enough."

Once she had left the room, silence fell for a moment. Neither Patience or Daniel had noticed, however, a figure lurking behind a nearby door; now Anne leaned out to look toward the pantry, and there were tears in her eyes as she thought back to everything she had just heard. On top of all the anguish and pain that she had endured, she now knew that her grandmother was not really her grandmother at all, that she had been lied to throughout her life.

Filled with anger, she slipped out of the room and then out of the house. She hurried across the yard, and then – once she was sure nobody had spotted her – she raced along the empty street.

CHAPTER EIGHTEEN

"WHAT'S THE MATTER HERE?" Daniel asked a few minutes later, as he rounded the corner and found a small congregation in the street outside *The Shoemaker*. "What is the cause of all this noise?"

"Look who was found barely outside the village," John Constable sneered, gesturing toward the grassy embankment opposite, where around two dozen men had gathered at the foot of the village's hanging post. "Looks like those American sympathizers were in the area after all."

"What are you talking about?" Daniel muttered, pushing through the crowd before stopping as soon as he saw a shivering, clearly injured man sitting on the grass with a noose already around his neck, connected to the top of the hanging post high above. "Who is this man?"

"He's admitted everything," Robert Domby said, standing behind the man and giving him a brief, hard kick. "This fellow is George Jones, one of the two men everyone has been searching for over the past week. He and his associate Thomas Vowles arrived in England recently, from the American colonies, and they're suspected of stealing a quantity of explosives that might be used to kill the king."

"Is this right?" Daniel asked, stepping closer to George. "Are you the man they describe?"

"What if I'm not?" George snarled up at him. "Would that make any difference? You mean to hang me either way."

"If you are an innocent man," Daniel replied, "then it would be as well to speak the truth."

"I found him on the road that leads to the north of here," Matthew Lopton said. "I was out searching for my father again."

"Has he absconded yet another time from that asylum?" John Constable asked.

"Aye," Matthew replied, "and I must go and search for him some more, but I discovered this fellow crawling about on the ground and I quickly became suspicious. I brought him here, and he was babbling all the way about some woman he claims did many grievous things to his person."

"He looks to have been badly hurt," Daniel

pointed out.

"Could a woman really do such harm?" Stockton Bart asked.

"She might," Daniel said, stepping around the man so as to get a better look at him, "if she was so inclined. Tell me, Mr. Jones, where is your co-conspirator? Where is Thomas Vowles?"

"I have nothing to say to any of you," George said darkly. "Why beg for my life when I already know what you're going to do?"

"He must be nearby," Robert Domby suggested, his voice dripping with disdain. "They'd hardly have separated, not when everyone has been searching for them high and low."

"I have made my peace with God," George said, "and that is enough for me. What I have seen these past twenty-four hours has shaken my faith to its core, yet I have remained strong. I escaped from that dreaded woman and now I can go to my grave, knowing that the spirit of revolution shall live on."

"There's no sign of the explosives," Stockton pointed out. "That Vowles man must have them."

"Where have you been hiding?" Daniel asked once he'd walked all the way around George. Stopping, he looked down at him again and saw the fear and anger in his eyes. "There aren't many places that might be appropriate around here, so tell me where you and your sniveling companion have made your base."

"Why would I do anything to help you?" George asked.

"Because I fear greatly that I already know the answer," Daniel told him.

"Where?" Stockton asked, stepping closer. "If you know, then say its name so that we can go and haul out the other miscreant. The only thing better than hanging one of them today would be to get them both up there!"

"Tell me where you have been hiding," Daniel said, still watching George carefully. "In the name of all that is holy, I pray that I'm wrong, yet..."

He paused, before stepping around him again while peering at the candlestick embedded in his shoulder. Although he still desperately wanted to believe that he was wrong, he felt that he recognized this particular candlestick and that it might well be the final proof that he required. Crouching down, he reached out and grabbed the candlestick's end, and now he was sure that he had seen this exact item before.

"Has this man been interrogated?" he asked.

"He hasn't exactly been very helpful," one of the other men murmured. "The only thing we need to know is where his friend might be with all those explosives."

"I think we know that already," Daniel replied, adjusting his grip on the candlestick as he looked into George's defiant eyes. "There's no point dragging this out further."

With that, he twisted the candlestick and pulled it out with one firm tug. Letting out a gasp of pain, George fell back and clutched his shoulder as fresh blood began to gush from the wound. He reached to grab the candlestick, but Daniel stepped back and watched calmly as several other men grabbed George by the arms and hauled him to his feet.

"Should we do it, then?" Morton Thatch asked.

"Do it," Daniel said firmly.

"But if we wait for -"

"Do it!" Daniel said again, as he watched George starting to struggle. "Let this wretch hurry on to Hell."

"You're all going to die!" George shouted as a few of the men began to pull the rope on the other side of the post. "You understand that, don't you? You're all on the wrong side of history and you're going to pay the ultimate price!" He struggled again as the rope tightened around his neck and began to lift him up. "Do you think you can stand in the way of progress? Your rotten king is going to lead you all to -"

Suddenly gasping as he was dragged up into the air, he reached for the rope and tried to pull it away from his neck as he let out a series of spluttering cries. At the same time he started kicking wildly, causing the gathered crowd to step back a little and watch from further back as the dying man struggled for breath.

"This is a common way to die in these parts, it would seem," Daniel observed, keeping his gaze fixed firmly on the man's bulging eyes. "I must confess, it seems to take longer than I had anticipated."

"We could pull on his legs and try to finish him off faster," John Constable suggested.

"And show mercy?" Daniel replied, glancing at him. "I would remind you that this man and his friend meant to kill our king. They are fighting on the side of those who would tear the colonies away from England's bosom, and what might happen then? Chaos, that is what. The American colonies have absolutely no hope of a strong future if they are not closely tied to our shores. Those who would sow the seeds of division must be made to pay a high price."

He looked back up at George, who was still battling ferociously to get free from the noose, although after a few seconds the man's struggles seemed to become a little weaker.

"There's still the other one to track down," Morton Thatch pointed out. "Where -"

"I know exactly where we can find him," Daniel said darkly as he continued to watch

George's dying throes. "And likely his explosives, too."

"Where?"

"Isn't it obvious? Where else could two rotten fugitives hide near Cobblefield?"

"In the forest?"

Daniel turned to him.

"In the... fields?" Morton suggested cautiously.

Daniel sighed.

"Then where?" Morton asked. "There's nowhere else, not unless -"

Stopping himself just in time, he finally realized the truth. As George continued to gasp for some last remaining breath, Morton watched Daniel with a growing sense of horror.

"I mean, the only other place," he said cautiously, "would be..."

"Exactly," Daniel said firmly. "Hadlow House." He looked over at the rest of the crowd, but he knew they were too far away and too engrossed in George's dying moments to listen, so when he turned to the other men he understood that in that moment only half a dozen pairs of ears could hear him. "And before anyone points out the obvious," he continued, "it is true that I promised my wife that I would help keep people away from that place for the rest of our lives."

"Then what do you propose we do?" Morton

asked.

Daniel hesitated, but deep down he already knew the answer.

"For the king," he said firmly, "and for our country, we must make haste to go out there and catch the remaining traitor. And I shall come with you, but I beg of each man here... I do not want my wife to know where we are going. Can you promise me that?"

Above them, as they continued their discussion, George Jones had finally fallen still. His dead body hung from the rope, and his bulging eyes were almost bursting from their sockets as a gentle breeze caused the corpse to sway in the wind.

CHAPTER NINETEEN

SLIPPING PAST THE EDGE of the village, Anne made sure to avoid the group of men – and some women – gathered over on the grass opposite the inn. She had seen a man's body hanging from the post, and this was the first time she had ever witnessed the post being used for its intended purpose. She had lingered to watch for a while, keen to see for the first time a man's death, but now she knew she had to make haste.

"Those girls are so lucky to have had you in their lives," she heard her grandfather's voice saying, ringing in her thoughts, "and while you might not be of the same blood, you have been a mother and a grandmother to them."

"If she knew -" her supposed grandmother had replied.

"She will never find out," her grandfather had added.

Yet now she knew the truth, and as she hurried along the grass verge at the side of the road leading northwards out of the village, Anne felt as if she had suffered the greatest possible betrayal. She had always loved her grandmother, and despite some arguments over the years she had obeyed her precisely because she believed that they were bound together by blood. Now, however, she understood that Patience Purkiss was not her real grandmother at all, that she was just some old woman who had somehow tricked her way into the family's life. With tears in her eyes, Anne felt as if she wanted to scream, but she knew that screaming would do no good.

And now the sight of that dead man, hanging from a rope, filled her thoughts and made her realize that life could be crueler and harsher than she had ever imagined.

Hearing voices, she realized that she was in danger of being spotted. Her grandmother – or rather, Patience – believed her to be in her room, but she knew that eventually her absence would be noticed. She wanted Patience to be worried, she wanted her to feel awful for that terrible slap, she wanted to punish her; for that to work, however, she needed to get away from the village for a while, and as she scurried along the road that led out of the village she knew that there was one place she could go that would really upset Patience.

She wasn't entirely sure where to find the mysterious Hadlow House, about which she'd heard so much, but she knew it was somewhere in the forest.

***

"But why must *you* go?" Patience asked for the third – perhaps even fourth – time as she sat at the kitchen table. "Daniel, I don't understand."

"All the men of the village are going out to hunt for this traitor," he told her as he set his pistol on the table. "I can't leave them to do the job alone."

"You're seventy-five years old," she pointed out. "Don't take this the wrong way, Daniel, but what use are you going to be? Leave this chase to the younger men! Do you even know where you're going to look?"

"Just around," he replied, checking the pistol while making sure to avoid meeting his wife's gaze. He knew he couldn't afford to give even the slightest hint that the traitor Vowles was at Hadlow House, for he worried that Patience would do anything short of killing him in order to keep him away from that place. "We're going to be heading south," he lied. "That's where Jones said his friend had gone."

"And this Jones fellow," she said, her voice tense with fear, "is he still hanging opposite the inn?"

"He is."

"How long will he be left there?"

"The sight of his wretched corpse will serve as a deterrent for a good while."

"I do wish he could be cut down tonight, at least," she muttered, shaking her head. "I'm sure you understand why I don't like to see such things."

"I'm sure something will be done tomorrow."

"But you're too old for this!" she snapped suddenly, getting to her feet as if filled with some fresh sense of worry. Hurrying around the table, she grabbed him by the arm. "I won't let you go!"

"*Let* me?"

"I'm your wife and I demand that you stay. Why, if this dangerous fellow Vowles is on the prowl, how do you know that he won't come to our home tonight? You need to stay here and protect your family."

"Patience -"

"Anne is asleep upstairs and I am defenseless!"

"There's nothing defenseless about you," he pointed out. "Patience, I have seen you fight the dead."

"I'm not joking!" she hissed.

"And I am not about to look like a coward!" he roared angrily. "Patience, I have indulged your paranoid fears for long enough, but that night at Hadlow House was more than fifty years ago! In fact, the more time passes, the more I wonder whether you merely influenced me to see things that weren't even there!"

"Influenced you?" she replied, shocked by his outburst. "What..."

Her voice trailed off as she stared at him, and after a few seconds she took a step back as she felt her knees threatening to buckle beneath her weight.

"Daniel," she stammered, "are you saying that you don't think that house is haunted after all?"

"I don't know what I think," he replied, "not anymore."

"But you saw it all!" she hissed. "You saw Fanny Baxter's ghost!"

"Did I?" he asked. "Or was I just so caught up in it all that I allowed you to make me *think* that I saw such ungodly things? I'm sorry, Patience, but I was an impressionable young fool and I was falling in love with you, and when I look back now I find myself contemplating the possibility that we were both mistaken! Can't you let that thought into your mind for even a moment? What if we were just so young, and so scared and so upset... that we fooled ourselves into blaming ghosts for perfectly normal events?"

"I can't believe that I'm hearing this," she said, as a tear ran down her cheek. "After everything that happened, I always believed that at least you were on my side."

"Of course I'm on your side," he said firmly, as he glanced at the window and realized that he'd already taken too long fetching his pistol. Soon the others would be marching out to Hadlow House. "I have always been on your side."

"But you think I am a fool?"

"I think we were both so young," he replied, turning to her again. "Your mother had died."

"Fanny Baxter murdered her!"

"Your father tried to kill you."

"Because he was under her influence!"

"I remember what I thought I saw at the time," he told her, "and what I believed, but I have to ask myself now whether that was all an illusion." He paused, before stepping toward her and putting a hand on the side of her arm, only for her to instantly pull away. "Can't you meet me halfway on this, Patience?" he asked. "I don't mean to doubt you, but occasionally I've found myself wondering what really happened to us back when we were young. And I would be lying if I said that I haven't had doubts about the more... unholy side of it all."

He waited for an answer, before touching

her arm again, only for her to once more pull away.

"You should go," she said bitterly, struggling to hold back more tears. "You wouldn't want to disappoint all the other men and make them fear that you're a coward."

"Patience -"

"And I'm glad to know what you really think," she added through gritted teeth. "You are only being honest at last, Daniel, and I have no right to feel anything other than grateful."

"We'll talk more when I get back," he told her, taking his pistol and heading to the door. "Keep Anne safe and don't be worried if I'm a little late back. One way or another, we're going to catch the other traitor and make sure that he can't go through with his heinous plan."

Patience listened to the sound of his footsteps walking away, followed by the bump of the front door. Finally accepting that he was gone, she slumped back down onto the chair and put her hands over her face, and the tears flowed freely down her face. Great convulsive sobs shook her body, and it was all she could do to keep from crying out with a ferocity that she worried might even wake Anne upstairs. As she replayed Daniel's doubting words over and over, she felt as if her heart was breaking at the realization that her husband – the one man upon whom she had always relied so very much – now doubted that Hadlow

House was haunted at all.

CHAPTER TWENTY

LETTING OUT A SHOCKED gasp – followed by a burp – Thomas Vowles rolled onto his side and found himself staring at a small battered table next to the bed.

For a moment, not quite knowing what had happened, he simply stared at the table. Finally his mind emerged from the fog of a deep sleep and he remembered that he was at Hadlow House in Kent, and that he'd settled down for a nap after returning to the house earlier. Sitting up, he remembered the old man on the street, and he sighed again as he remembered killing the man and finding that he was carrying nothing more valuable than a few stupid pebbles. He took a moment to wipe some sweat from his brow, and then – spotting a flickering light on the landing beyond the bedroom's door – he got to his feet and stumbled over to take a closer look.

"George?" he called out. "Is that you? Are you back?"

Hearing no answer, he stepped out onto the landing and made his way to the top of the stairs. He remembered now that upon his return, Mrs. Baxter had presented him with yet another feast. Feeling a faint pain in his right arm, he rubbed the spot just above the shoulder just as he let out yet another hot, heavy fart; a kind of heaviness was weighing his gut down, but he supposed that this was entirely natural given the huge amount of food he'd consumed since Mrs. Baxter had started taking care of him.

"George?" he shouted. "Mrs. Baxter?"

Still hearing nothing by way of reply, he headed to the top of the stairs and then began to walk down. He tottered slightly, feeling a little weak, and then as he reached the hallway he saw that the fireplace in the old study was roaring. Turning, he looked toward the dining room and saw the same thing in that room as well, and then he realized that there was also a glow coming from the kitchen. He remembered that George had warned him not to light the house up too much, lest attention be drawn to the place, and as he shuffled through to the kitchen he wondered whether anything might be amiss.

"There you are," Fanny said, suddenly

stepping into the doorway and smiling at him. "You're just in time for supper."

"Supper?" he replied. "I'm terribly sorry, but I'm not sure that I can eat anything at all."

He rubbed his belly, which felt a little swollen.

"I'm not -"

Before he could finish, he heard the sound of a chair's leg scraping against wood in the dining room. He looked over his shoulder and found himself wondering whether George might be in there.

"Ignore that," Fanny said firmly.

"George?" He limped to the door and looked into the dining room, and he was surprised to see that there was no sign of anyone.

"Mr. Vowles, please," Fanny continued, sounding a little annoyed now, "you must come to the kitchen for a moment. The dining room is so overrated in this house. I believe that a good meal can be served perfectly adequately in the kitchen."

"You do, do you?"

He turned to her, and he couldn't escape the feeling that something was very wrong.

"Is George back yet?"

"Does that matter?"

"A great deal, for he and I..." He hesitated, aware that he really shouldn't tell her too much. "Well, it's complicated," he added, "but I really need to know that he's alright."

"He's perfectly alright."

"How do you know that?"

"Because he came back a short while ago," she explained with a faint, slightly pained smile, "and he said that he needed to fetch some more supplies for your terribly important mission, and then he left again."

"He did?"

She nodded. "He did."

"Oh." Thomas thought about this for a moment. He had wanted to ask George a number of questions, but he realized now that he couldn't help the fact that he'd been asleep for several hours. "Well, I suppose I can't argue with that," he muttered. "Did he say where he was going?"

"Just out."

"And what of the fires? I'm not sure they should be lit. What if somebody sees them and comes to investigate who is staying at this house?"

"You really mustn't concern yourself about such things," Fanny told him, and now her smile seemed much more genuine. "Please, come and sit down so that I can give you some nice food. After all, you want to be big and strong, don't you? And don't worry about the lights." She looked over at the flames in the kitchen's fireplace, and then at the darkened window at the far end of the room. "I'm sure they won't attract anything more interesting than a few stray beasts."

***

As some more twigs cracked and splintered beneath her feet, Anne made her way through the pitch-black forest while hugging herself for warmth. She hadn't really thought ahead very much, and she certainly had never expected the forest to be so cold.

A moment later, however, she spotted a faint flickering light in the distance. Stopping for a moment, she felt her heart skip a beat as she began to wonder exactly what might be lurking ahead, and then she realized that she might actually have found the mysterious Hadlow House. She had been searching for several hours, keen to locate the house that caused Patience so much grief, but now she felt a tightening sense of fear in her chest as she realized that she might actually have to be brave.

She set off again, picking her way through the undergrowth until she emerged at the edge of the clearing. With darkness having fallen now, she saw what appeared to be a wall running around the edge of the property, with a metal gate a little further along.

After taking a deep breath, she stepped forward, only to flinch and turn as she heard a rustling sound. To her immense relief, she saw that the source of this sound was a horse tethered to a nearby post.

"You scared me," she told the horse, feeling a little silly now.

Once she'd managed to regather her composure, she began to creep toward the large metal gate. Looking up, she was just about able to see the name Hadlow House in large letters over the top, and then she stopped to look between the bars. Sure enough, she saw a fairly large house with flickering firelight visible in a couple of the windows, and she immediately furrowed her brow as she realized that fires in the hearths could only mean that people were in the house.

She swallowed hard, before gently pushing the gate open and stepping into the garden.

As she walked along the path that led to the house's front door, she felt as if she was leaving the rest of the world further and further behind. She also felt a growing sense of fear in her chest, and she realized after a moment that she was watching the windows as if she expected to spot a figure at any moment. She wasn't sure who she expected to encounter, exactly, but she had overheard Patience talking many times about someone named Fanny. Evidently this had been 'grown-up talk' to which Anne hadn't been privy, but she found herself wondering what kind of person could possibly live in such a remote and imposing house.

Occasionally she'd heard Patience talking about ghosts and spirits, but she felt quite sure that such things weren't even real.

Suddenly she spotted movement at one of the downstairs windows. Panicked, she rushed forward and threw herself onto the ground directly beneath that window, and then she held her breath for a few seconds before forcing herself to look up. She could see the glow at the window, but after a few more seconds a dark shadow also appeared and she was just about able to make out the face of an old woman staring out across the garden.

Supposing that she hadn't been spotted yet, Anne stayed as still as possible until – a moment later – the old woman slowly pulled back out of sight.

"What do you mean, you went out to Hadlow House?" she imagined Patience shouting angrily. "Are you insane? I expressly ordered you never to do that! Why would you disobey me like this?"

A shiver passed through Anne's body as she realized that this was precisely the reaction she wanted. And for that to happen, she was going to have to convincingly explain that she'd done more than simply peer through a window. If she was going to truly infuriate Patience, she'd need to actually go inside the house, so slowly and carefully she began to crawl along the edge of the wall, searching for some way to get inside.

CHAPTER TWENTY-ONE

ALL THE CHESS PIECES were in place.

Sitting alone at the kitchen table, Patience Purkiss stared at the board and thought back to the last time she'd played a game with her granddaughter. Chess had somehow became their favorite shared hobby, a way to pass the time but also a way to prove to themselves – if to no-one else – that their minds were sharp. Anne had showed great talent for chess, to the extent that Patience sometimes thought she might even be able to beat a man, although she knew that she should keep such absurd thoughts to herself.

Now, as she stared at the pieces that had been left midway through the most recent game, she realized that she needed a distraction from the argument with Daniel. Her thoughts were swarming and she longed for the days when she had been able to empty her mind and focus exclusively on the here and now.

"Anne?" she called out, looking at the open door that led into the hallway. "Anne, are you asleep? If not, would you like to come and finish our game?"

She waited.

"I know it's late," she continued, imagining the little girl listening from her bedroom upstairs, "but I think that just this once you can be allowed to come down. I shan't even tell your grandfather, he doesn't have to know if you're up late once in a while. We could simply play a game or two until our minds are tired. Wouldn't you like that?"

Again she waited, and now she was starting to worry that the child might actually be asleep. That was a good thing, she knew, but at the same time she desperately wanted to prove that she really wasn't *still* angry, so after a few seconds she got to her feet and made her way out into the hallway, and then she stopped to look up the stairs.

The house was completely silent.

Was Anne asleep after all?"

"Anne?" she said, raising her voice just a little higher than before. "There's no need to be afraid. I'm just offering you the chance to come and play a game of chess with me, that's all."

She heard no answer.

"Won't you please come?" she asked plaintively, no longer even trying to hide the sense of loneliness in her voice. "You'd be doing me a wonderful favor."

As she continued to wait, Patience began to worry that she was being selfish. After all, what right did she have to wake a young girl up in the middle of the night and ask her to play a game of chess? Deep down she felt sure that she should simply turn around and go back to the kitchen, and that she should let Anne sleep while waiting dutifully for Daniel's return. Then she and Daniel would discuss the earlier argument in a civilized manner, like adults, and she felt sure that they'd be able to swiftly get over their differences. Yet, in her heart, she so desperately wanted to have Anne with her in the kitchen, so as to not be alone.

"I'm coming up," she said softly, before starting to make her way up the stairs. "I'm sorry if I have to wake you but -"

Stopping suddenly, she flinched as she realized that the scratching sound had returned. Standing on the third step, she told herself that she had to be wrong, that the sound was something else, yet even now she could feel a faint itching sensation in her left ear, as if this might be the source of the scratching. She reached up and touched the side of her ear, but now the sound seemed to be almost trying to pull her back, and as she turned and looked toward the front door she realized that she was being drawn out into the village. In that moment, in her mind's eye, she thought of Fanny Baxter's grave in the cemetery.

For a fraction of a second she considered ignoring the sound and going up to Anne, but her resolve was too weak; reasoning that Anne would be fine alone for an hour or so, she instead hurried to the front door and slipped out into the night.

***

By the time she reached the steps leading up into the cemetery, carrying the shovel she'd borrowed from the yard, Patience was a little out of breath but no less determined to get to the truth.

She reached for the railing as she headed up to the top step, and then she paused for a moment to look around the cemetery and try to get her bearings. Moonlight was catching the tops of the gravestones, but a few seconds later her attention was caught by something else entirely as she looked beyond the cemetery's low stone wall and saw a shape hanging from the post opposite *The Shoemaker*. The body of George Jones had been left as a warning to all those who might witness such a sorry sight, and for a moment Patience found that she couldn't turn away from the ghastly vision.

As a low breeze blew through the night air,

she thought she could just about see the body swinging slightly in the wind. She knew that George Jones and his associate were wicked, of course, yet she still couldn't shake the feeling that there was something so macabre about having a dead body dangling on full display in the middle of the village.

After making the sign of the cross against her chest, she turned and carried the shovel across the cemetery. She spotted her father's freshly-dug grave, but she had no time to stop; already she was heading toward the cemetery's far end, and she could see Fanny's grave in the moonlight. She almost tripped a few times on the rough, uneven grass, and she inadvertently banged the shovel's side against a couple of gravestones, but finally she stopped and looked down at one stone in particular, bearing the name of Frances Baxter.

And the scratching sound was now so loud in her ears that she caught herself flinching slightly.

"Do you think I don't know it's you?" she snapped angrily. "Do you think me a complete fool?"

She waited for a moment, before looking down at the grass. On her way to the cemetery she'd been going over various plans, but now she realized that the time had come for action. She knew that Fanny's coffin was down there in the darkness, that the woman's body had been rotting for more than half a century. Somewhere in the back of her mind, a sane and rational voice was questioning whether she was making the right decision and telling her to go home to Anne, but that voice was quickly drowned out by the realization that she had to end the scratching sound once and for all. She also felt that if she could destroy the body of Fanny Baxter, she might yet be able to end the dead woman's reign of terror.

"I'm coming for you," she sneered, and then – without further thought – she pushed the shovel's head into the ground and began to dig. "As the Lord is my witness, I shall not stop until you are gone!"

She quickly found that her arms were a little too weak for such a huge job, but she told herself that she simply had to keep pushing. Glancing around to make sure that nobody else was up and about on such a dark and strange night, she somehow managed to keep digging with ferocious intensity, eventually dropping into a kind of trance as she tried desperately to get down to the coffin that she knew must be waiting six feet below.

Then five feet.

Then four.

Three.

Two.

Suddenly she felt the shovel's tip hit something hard. Startled, she took a step back; all sense of time had deserted her, to the extent that she had no idea how long she had spent digging, but her arms were burning with pain and she let out an angry grunt as she finally threw the shovel aside. Crouching down, she began to use her fingers to move the last of the dirt aside, and soon she was able to make out the lid of the coffin. A tightening sense of anticipation was starting to fill her chest but she knew that she couldn't stop now, she felt sure that this was the only way to truly rid the world of Fanny Baxter's malign presence once and for all.

Entirely distracted by this task, she could think of nothing and no-one else as she finally exposed the coffin's lid. Reaching around the side, she fumbled for a moment to work out how to pull it away, but she quickly realized that there were no nails or pins holding it in place; that was a stroke of luck, for she had brought nothing that might aid her in breaking into the coffin itself, and after a moment she shifted around so that she was straddling the coffin and then she began to pull the lid up.

The scratching sound continued as the lid creaked and groaned. And then, just as Patience pulled the lid aside, the scratching came to an abrupt halt.

Letting out a shocked gasp, Patience held the lid out of the way and stared down into the coffin. Bathed in moonlight, the bones of Fanny Baxter lay waiting; her skull's empty eye-sockets stared up, seemingly watching Patience as she realized that the time had come to make everything right.

CHAPTER TWENTY-TWO

A DOZEN MEN MOVED through the darkness, picking their way along the pitch-black road that led through the forest. And then, as one of the men at the front raised a hand to stop them all, they spotted a faint flickering light up ahead.

"That's it," Joshua Marsden said. "Is it not?"

"It is," Daniel replied, his heart filled with fear as he saw the place again for the first time in more than fifty years. "Everyone stay close and be careful. We must move with great care. That is indeed Hadlow House, but we must hold back for a moment and come up with a plan. After all, if Thomas Vowles is in there, he is most certainly armed."

***

"You have outdone yourself yet again, Mrs. Baxter," Thomas could be heard saying in the house's dining room, speaking even though his mouth was full. "I honestly don't know when you find the time to cook such magnificent feasts. It's almost like sorcery!"

"You must not concern yourself with such thoughts," Fanny replied calmly. "Truly, your only task tonight, Sir, is to eat and be hearty."

"I'm still worried about George," he muttered, before letting out a loud burp. "It's really not like him to be gone for so long. We have a very important plan that we must -"

He let out another burp, although this time it came with a brief, punching pain pushing up through his chest. He winced as he felt a strange sensation, almost as if his breastbone had shifted a little.

"We have a very important plan," he continued, "and it's essential that we -"

He burped again, and this time he could no longer hide the pain at all. Feeling a little breathless now, he reached up and wiped sweat from his brow.

"It's essential that we proceed swiftly," he added, struggling now to get the words out at all. "Any delay will only add confusion, and we have worked so hard to get to this point. We have made so many sacrifices, we have lost so many friends, but it will all be worth the effort if we just get the job done. God is -"

Yet another burp shook his body, and he let out a brief cry of pain.

"God is on our side," he murmured, before farting heavily. "The world is on our side. We are the future and soon the whole of humanity will see that."

He hesitated, only for yet another burp to shake his body, shooting upward as if borne on the wings of many knives. Leaning forward, he took a moment to try to pull himself together, and then he slipped some more meat into his mouth in the hope that this would force the unpleasantness back down.

"We are on the side of right," he said, "against the side of wrong. That will surely see us through eventually. I just need George to get back here so that we can get on with things."

On her hands and knees just inside the kitchen door, having crept into the house without making a sound, Anne listened to the voices. She knew that she might be making a mistake, and that she was most certainly going against her grandmother's wishes, but at the same time she wanted to prove – to herself, and also to the whole wide world – that she was brave enough to do such a thing. She'd heard the voices as soon as she'd entered the house, and now that she'd crawled past the edge of the counter she was just about able to make out what they were saying.

"I'm such a glutton," Thomas muttered, with his mouth still packed full of food, "but how can any man resist when the feast is so magnificent? Mrs. Baxter, I fear I must ask you to stop tempting me with such things."

"You *need* your strength," she told him. "That's what I always used to say to my dear Oliver.

"And he was your husband, I believe?"

"He died a long time ago."

"I'm sorry."

"There is no need to be," she replied. "He fell victim to a moment of foolishness that was visited upon him by... somebody else. By a woman named Catherine Hadlow, as it happens. He went climbing up that old oak tree outside with a saw and... Well, let us just say that he became confused while he was up there. Not that Catherine Hadlow can be blamed entirely, of course. At the end of the day, we are all solely responsible for our own actions."

"Did he fall?"

"Not exactly," she said cautiously, "but you really don't need to concern yourself with such matters. How many times do I have to tell you, you need only worry about what is right in front of you."

"This meat is sublime," he muttered. "It's like nothing I've ever eaten before."

Feeling more than a little curious, and reasoning that she could turn and run at any moment, Anne crawled further across the floor, slowly approaching the open doorway that led through into the hall. She stopped and and listened, and this time she was about to hear a slow and rather disgusting chewing sound, as if somebody was feasting happily. She saw an open doorway leading into another room, and after a moment she was able to make out a shadow dancing against the wall in the glow of a flickering fire.

"Make sure not to waste any," Fanny said soothingly. "You know, if there's one thing I really don't like in all the world, Mr. Vowles, it's waste."

"I shan't be wasting any of this magnificent meat," he replied, "although I fear I might have to waste these trousers if my girth increases. That's a little play on words, by the way."

"Yes, I understand perfectly."

Anne watched the open doorway, and somehow the chewing, sucking sound seemed to be getting louder and louder.

"Mr. Vowles," Fanny continued, "I must attend to a few other matters. If you don't mind, I shall leave you to get on with things here while I go upstairs."

"That's absolutely fine by me," he told her. "But are you really *sure* you don't want to eat? I wouldn't mind at all if you were to join me!"

"Again, that is a very kind offer, but I really don't think that it would be appropriate. Besides, I don't have much of an appetite these days." Footsteps headed toward the open door, and a moment later a woman's silhouetted figure appeared in view.

Anne immediately pulled back a little, preparing herself to run if necessary.

"It's so nice to have people to look after," Fanny said, watching George once more. "I really think it's my one purpose in all existence. I just wish everyone could be as grateful as you are, Mr. Vowles. Unfortunately I find that as the world progresses, simple qualities such as gratitude are going terribly out of fashion. Wouldn't you agree?"

"You're sure that the fires are a good idea, aren't you?" he asked cautiously. "It's just that George thought we should avoid attracting -"

"There's nothing to worry about," she said firmly, cutting him off. "All the way out here, who is going to even be aware of a few flames flickering in the hearths of Hadlow House? Please, Mr. Vowles, eat heartily and I shall be back down shortly. I just need to be alone for a few minutes so that I might... concentrate on an urgent matter. I'm afraid that something elsewhere has been begging for my attention for quite some time, and there is only so long I can wait before I deal with the matter."

Anne watched as the woman walked toward the bottom of the stairs. Before she could go up, however, Fanny stopped with her back toward the kitchen door, and then she slowly began to turn and look over her shoulder.

Terrified that she might be spotted, Anne pulled back but she somehow refrained from making her escape. She told herself that the woman was merely looking around and that there was no need to be concerned, and a moment later this assumption was shown to be correct as she heard the sound of Fanny slowly making her way up the staircase. Looking at the ceiling, Anne heard the woman going into one of the bedrooms, followed by the sound of a door swinging shut.

From the dining room, meanwhile, there still came the sound of Thomas Vowles ferociously and eagerly chomping his way through meat.

Picturing a hugely fat man with meat juices dribbling down his chin, Anne realized that she desperately wanted to actually *see* this fellow for herself. She knew that she'd be taking a little extra risk, but she also knew that the housekeeper was upstairs, so after a moment she very carefully got to her feet and took a step forward into the hallway. She told herself that she would turn and run at the first hint that the strange woman from upstairs might be coming down again, but as she tip-toed toward the door she felt a newfound sense of bravery.

"You're just a child," she remembered Patience having told her a few days earlier. "There's so much of the adult world that you still don't understand."

"Your grandmother is right," her grandfather had replied. "Anne, you are at that awkward age where you think that you're old enough to know better, whereas in fact you are still so very innocent."

"I'll show you," she whispered under her breath. "You're wrong about me."

After glancing at the ceiling and making sure that there was still no suggestion of Fanny returning, she took one more step forward and began to peer around the corner. Despite the sense of fear that was growing in her belly, she told herself that she was simply going to look at the strange man and then retreat. After a moment she spotted him, and she saw that he was sitting at the far end of a long table.

In front of the man, a mass of meat lay on the table with scraps littered all across the surface. Anne had never seen so much meat in all her life, and she couldn't help but notice that the man seemed to be eating with frantic intensity. She'd assumed that he was going to be big and fat, yet instead she saw that he was a rather thin man, although as she squinted slightly she realized that she really couldn't quite make him out properly. Something was wrong, yet for a few more seconds she couldn't work out why the entire scene seemed so discomforting. She watched as the man chewed on some more meat, with fresh blood dribbling from his lips, and then her eyes opened wide with horror as she saw him reaching down with his fork and digging away at the meat on his plate.

His own arm.

The man was sitting seemingly contentedly, showing no sign of pain as he scratched and cut away at the meat of his own left arm, which was already covered in blood with glistening lengths of exposed bone.

Suddenly the man looked up at Anne, and in that moment she could only scream.

AMY CROSS

CHAPTER TWENTY-THREE

STANDING IN THE GRAVE, Patience Purkiss continued to stare down at the bones of Fanny Baxter. There was no meat left on the woman's body at all, and the sight was more or less exactly as Patience had expected, yet she couldn't help staring at the skull.

"Can you see me?" she whispered, even though she felt terribly foolish for uttering the question. "Can you hear me? Is this really you?"

She waited, and although she hardly dared to imagine that the bones might conspire to give her an answer, she still couldn't quite shake the feeling that she was in some way once again in Fanny's presence. She looked around once more, just in case there might be any sign of the ghostly woman, and then – supposing that she needed to do something now that the corpse was exposed – she climbed into the coffin and crouched down to take a closer look.

Spotting some scratches on the inside of the coffin's lid, she leaned forward. She had to run her fingertips against the scratches to make them out, but they seemed almost to form – twice – the letter H.

"You're not so fearsome now, are you?" she asked, peering back down at the skull. "I have lived in fear of you for more than fifty years, ever since that night. You have dogged my nightmares, even my waking thoughts at times. I have pretended otherwise, even to myself, yet in truth I'm not sure that I have ever been able to entirely escape your shadow. Until now. Do you remember how you tried to keep me in that house, and how I escaped by climbing up through the chimney?"

Again she waited, and then she surprised herself by reaching down and gently picking up the skull. The jawbone immediately fell away, but Patience felt that this was of no matter; it was the empty eye-sockets she wished to inspect more closely, and she found herself staring into these two dark gaps as if they were the most enormous chasms.

"And then you took my father," she continued, with a growing tension in her voice, "and you kept him here for all those years until there was almost nothing left of him. Did that satisfy you? Did you gain even a sliver of happiness from that victory, or do you always want more?"

She held the skull up a little higher.

"When," she added, "will you be content with what you have taken?"

***

Sitting alone in the darkness of one of Hadlow House's bedrooms, Fanny stared straight ahead into darkness. She had been looking at the hole in the wall, the same hole just above the fireplace through which she had grabbed Patience all those years ago, but now her gaze her lost its focus.

Downstairs a young girl's voice cried out, but Fanny showed no reaction at all. Instead she simply continued to stare at the wall as her hands rested on the bed. After a moment, a thick black beetle crawled across the bed and onto her hand.

***

"What do I have to do to make you stop?" Patience asked, tilting the skull a little. "Burn you? Crush you? Throw you into the sea?"

She waited, even though she expected no answer.

"You know you will never get me again, don't you?" she continued. "Nor will you ever get your hands on anyone from my family. There is no way that another Butler or Purkiss will *ever* set foot in that house again."

***

Back at the front room in the house in the village, the chessboard remained where it had been left, with all the pieces still in position.

***

"Help me!" Anne screamed, pulling back against the wall and then dropping to her feet as she stared in horror at the man at the far end of the table. "Somebody!"

"Who are you?" Thomas Vowles asked, slowly getting to his feet, letting his ravaged left arm hang down weakly as blood dribbled from the many wounds. "Young lady, would you like to join me in this feast? It's most sumptuous, and I believe that I have enough to share."

He looked down at the scraps of meat on the table.

"The presentation is -"

Stopping suddenly, he furrowed his brow as he saw the true horror of what had happened. Whereas previously his vision had been filled with imagined cuts of meat and delicately-arranged accompaniments, now he saw the truth, and a moment later he felt a burning pain in his arm. When he held the arm up, his eyes opened wider than ever as he saw that he had cut away almost all the meat and muscle, leaving only exposed bone.

"How is this possible?" he stammered, as Anne screamed again. "What have I done?"

***

Upstairs, Fanny Baxter continued to stare blankly at the hole in the wall, but this time a faint smile was slowly starting to reach her lips.

The black beetle, meanwhile, was now crawling up her arm and onto her shoulder.

***

"Did you hear that?" Jethro Mann asked, stopping in the bushes and looking across at the house. "Somebody cried out."

"Aye, but it could be a trap," Daniel warned him.

"It sounded like a woman to me," Jethro replied. "Barely that, even. Perhaps just a girl."

"We must wait," Daniel said firmly. "There might only be one of these miscreants left, but I refuse to countenance any further loss of life on account of this treason." He looked around at the other men. "We outnumber this fool by more than ten to one, but that doesn't mean he's not still dangerous."

"Then what would you have us do?" Josiah asked.

"Let us wait for one moment more," Daniel told him, "while we come up with the perfect plan. And when that is ready, we shall drag Thomas Vowles kicking and screaming out of Hadlow House."

"What about -"

Daniel turned to Adam Turner, who was watching him with a fearful expression.

"Well," Adam continued, "we've all heard the stories about this place. You yourself are married to Samuel Butler's daughter, and by all reckonings she was long ago at the center of the dark things that happened here. I don't mean to dig up old tales, Daniel, but you must admit that there are few men who would willingly go into that place."

"If you wish to be a coward," Daniel replied, "then so be it, but I shall never shy from doing the right thing. We all swore to defend our king and country, with our lives if necessary, and I happen to believe that those words mattered a great deal as they left our lips."

"What if -"

"There is no ghost here," he added, even

though he felt a tug of guilt in his heart as those words left his lips. "There never has been. It was all a moment of hysteria that occurred many years ago, and I will not let such foolishness stop us from doing our duties today." He turned to some of the other men. "Before we apprehend this villain, I want a show of hands. Who here is willing to do the right thing?"

He waited, and one by one the men raised their hands until all of them – even Adam Turner, in the end – had indicated that they were with him.

"So be it," Daniel said firmly. "Make sure your pistols are ready to fire, but we should try to capture Vowles alive if possible, so that he can name any further co-conspirators before he joins his accomplice George Jones hanging from the gallows in our fair village."

***

"What has happened?" Thomas gasped, stepping around the table before stopping as he felt his legs preparing to buckle beneath him. More and more blood was running from his injured arm, and his mouth hung open for a moment as if he genuinely could not comprehend everything that was happening around him.

Finally, with his remaining good hand, he reached out toward Anne as she shivered in fear in the corner.

"Please," he stammered, "you have to help me!"

***

Sitting on the bed in complete darkness, Fanny stared ahead and now the smile had grown across her face.

The beetle, meanwhile, had reached her chin and quickly scurried up over her cheek. Reaching her right eye, it hesitated for a moment before stepping onto the surface, and Fanny did not so much as blink or even flinch as the beetle began to dig its way into her eyeball. Within seconds the creature had made a large enough hole in the center of the dead woman's pupil, and it quickly climbed inside, disappearing from view and letting its tiny legs scratch into the eyeball's soft center as Fanny began to laugh.

***

"You'll never get anyone from my family again," Patience said firmly, still staring at the skull in her hand. "You might as well give up now. Do you hear me? Just leave my family alone and -"

Suddenly a large black beetle scurried out of the right eye-socket and dropped onto Patience's wrist. Startled, she let out a shocked cry and pulled back, dropping the skull and letting it fall down heavily into the coffin.

CHAPTER TWENTY-FOUR

"I DON'T UNDERSTAND," THOMAS groaned, as he reached out and leaned against the last chair for support, just about managing to hold himself up. "Please, I don't understand any of it. What..."

He stared down at Anne for a moment longer, before slowly turning and looking over his shoulder. For some time now he had been imagining himself feasting from great prime cuts of meat. He'd wondered how Mrs. Baxter was able to get such wonderful things, and how she managed to cook them so quickly and so easily, but any concerns or doubts had been quickly swept away by a rush of pure, sheer gluttony. More than anything else, he had greatly enjoyed every single mouthful, yet now all he saw were scraps of torn meat.

Looking at his own left arm, he furrowed his

brow as he marveled at the sight of long, gray section of bone surrounded by clumps of pink tissue. He just about managed to clench his fist and open it again, yet he still couldn't quite believe what was right before his eyes.

"They deceive me," he stammered. "My own eyes, and they are liars! This cannot be, this horror that I see before me, it cannot be the truth. The only explanation is that I am imagining things *now*! Not then! No, not then, but now! Do you understand? It's really the only thing that makes even the slightest lick of sense."

He turned to Anne again.

"Tell me, child, what do you observe when you look at me? Mark that you answer honestly, because this is a very important matter." He stepped forward and held his ravaged arm out toward her. "Tell me what you see!" he gasped as tears began to roll down his cheeks. "Tell me honestly! Tell me what I have become!"

Before Anne could scream again, they both heard the sound of a door opening upstairs. Looking out into the hallway, Anne listened to a series of footsteps; she knew she should run, but at the same time she was too terrified to move a muscle.

"That's her!" Thomas murmured, turning and limping out into the hallway. "She'll explain everything. She'll make it all right and -"

Stumbling, he slammed into the wall and

barely managed to stay on his feet. After a moment he forced himself to keep going, and he reached the bottom of the stairs just as Fanny calmly made her way down.

"Mrs. Baxter," Thomas said, "I must confess that I need your help a little. There seems to have been some kind of terrible misunderstanding, and I don't know if it's the surfeit of food or the worry about George, but I am having trouble quite getting my head around certain... developments."

He waited for a reply, but she was merely staring blankly at him.

"Your eye," he continued, peering at the spot where the beetle had disappeared into her ghostly form. "You seem to have picked up..."

He tried to work out exactly how to describe the wound, before shaking his head as he realized that this wasn't strictly necessary right now.

"Anyway," he said, "the point I think I'm trying to make is that I don't think I can quite trust what I think I'm seeing at the moment, so I would very much like to try to understand exactly what's happening." He hesitated, before holding his damaged left arm up for her to see. "I know this is going to sound like a strange question," he continued as more blood dribbled down onto the floor, "but I beg your indulgence for one moment. Pray, tell me... when you look at my left hand and arm, what do you see?"

She stared at the damaged arm for a moment, before looking him in the eye again.

"Madame, what do you see?" he asked, almost pleading with her to give him good news. "What... what has happened to my arm?"

"It would appear," she replied coolly, "that the vast majority of the flesh and skin and meat has been cut away. At first you were quite happy eating some carefully selected pieces from your friend Mr. Jones, but after he departed this house I had to serve you your own body instead. I must confess, I thought you seemed perhaps unaware of what was happening, especially when you commented upon my cooking when – as you see now – everything you have eaten has been raw. Why, Mr. Vowles, during your feast what did you see?"

"I saw finely-cooked meat of the highest order," he told her, his voice filled with a sense of disbelief. "I saw meals fit for a king."

"But you are not a king, are you?"

"No, I -"

"So why would you have the meals of a king?" she asked sharply. "Besides, I had thought that you and Mr. Jones were not great admirers of King George. Has it not been your intention for some time now to go back up to London and in some manner... blow him up?"

"For the cause," Thomas said softly.

"The cause?"

"America," he replied, shaking his head slightly as if he was still coming to terms with everything happening around him. "But I digress..."

He looked at his arm again.

"This is not possible," he continued, as he began to blink wildly. "I cannot have been eating my own arm, I would surely have felt the pain."

"Yes, unless something blocked that."

"And I would have seen the horror."

"Indeed, unless for some reason you only saw what you *wanted* to see."

"Mrs. Baxter," he added, "I think I feel a little unwell."

"You certainly look very pale," she told him, tilting her head slightly. "Mr. Vowles, I really must be completely honest with you and admit that my mind is now on other matters. I believe I have been extremely hospitable since you arrived here at the house, but you really don't have any right to be here, do you?"

He opened his mouth to reply, but once again he was struck by a wave of weakness and all his strength was required for him to even stay on his feet.

"You are an interloper at Hadlow House," Fanny said firmly, "and while I have indulged you until this moment, I feel the time is soon coming to draw a line under this whole sorry episode. Mr. Vowles, I am the housekeeper here and while security is not usually part of my job description, I feel that I must take exception to the way you and your friend have abused the property. This sort of thing simply isn't on!"

"Can you help me?" he gasped as sweat began to run down his face. "I'm not -"

Suddenly hearing a scrabbling sound, he turned just in time to see Anne racing out of the dining room and rushing to the kitchen.

"Young girl," he said, turning to watch as she hurried away, "might you stop for a moment and help me?"

"She's trying to escape," Fanny sneered, as they both heard the sound of Anne desperately trying to get the back door open, "but I'm afraid she's going to find that all the doors and windows are sealed." She paused for a moment as the smile returned to her lips. "And I'm also afraid that, unlike her resourceful supposed grandmother, she's not going to be able to climb to freedom up the chimney. Which leaves her trapped in here with me, just as I had hoped might happen all along." She stepped past Thomas and began to make her way toward the kitchen. "A long time ago," she explained, "Patience Butler wronged me. It's time for her to learn that such rudeness simply will not do."

"I beg your assistance," Thomas replied, leaning against the wall as he tried to remain conscious. "Mrs. Baxter? Young girl? I really do need one of you to support me while I try to determine the best course of action."

Hearing Anne's scream ringing out from the kitchen, he turned and shuffled over to the foot of the stairs. A floorboard creaked beneath his left foot, and as he stopped and looked into the study he saw all the boxes of explosives that George had made him carry in from the cart. Taking a deep breath, he leaned against the jamb and tried to pull his thoughts together, but a moment later – as Anne screamed again – he realized that he could hear a faint scraping sound coming from somewhere outside, from beyond the window.

"What in the blazes is that?" he murmured, taking a step forward. "I really don't know what -"

Suddenly a gunshot rang out from somewhere in the garden, shattering the window and causing Thomas to cry out as he slumped down against the floor.

CHAPTER TWENTY-FIVE

"DID YOU GET HIM?" Adam Turner asked, keeping his voice low as he watched the broken window. "I saw him fall!"

"I don't think I actually hit the man," Joshua Marsden replied as he began to reload his pistol. "The cursed traitor ducked down just in time and now he knows we're here!"

"He's outnumbered and surrounded," Daniel pointed out as he looked across the garden. He couldn't see the other men, but he trusted that they had taken up their positions at various spots in the darkness and were waiting for the signal to advance. "We'll have him, alright, but I won't let him take the life of even one more honest Englishman."

"He's nothing but a coward!" Adam hissed.

"God is on our side!"

"We heard a cry," Daniel reminded them, "and it sounded to me like a girl. This particular coward would seem to have taken a hostage."

"But how?" Adam asked. "Who could ever have -"

"None of that matters right now," Daniel replied firmly. "What matters is that we get everyone out alive, and then we can deal with Vowles. We have already shown once this week what we do to traitorous scum, and I shall have no hesitation in showing that determination once more."

"Are you sure there's no -"

Jethro Mann hesitated for a moment, as if he knew that his next question was unwise.

"What I mean," he continued cautiously, "is that there have long been tales about this house. At least for as long as I've been alive, I've heard the whispers. We all have. Mr. Purkiss, I'm sure I speak for all the men when I say that we're glad to be led by you, but are you certain there's nothing unholy in that place?"

Daniel opened his mouth to reply, before looking once more at Hadlow House and thinking back to that night more than fifty years ago when he'd managed to rescue Patience and her father. At the time he'd fully believed everything Patience had told him about the ghostly Fanny Baxter, he even thought that he'd seen evidence, yet now he was an old man and the passage of time made him doubt all those certainties. The house looked gloomy and unwelcoming, and there was a certain dark atmosphere in the air, but now – so far removed from that one particular night – he found all his belief in ghostly visitations had drained away.

"There's nothing," he said finally, partly to reassure the men and partly to reassure himself. "Absolutely nothing. Now make sure that your pistols are loaded, for they shall surely soon be needed. We're going to take Thomas Vowles alive, and then we're going to make sure that he pays for what he's done. For, as you mentioned, we have God on our side."

***

"Lord, help me!" Thomas stammered, sobbing frantically as he checked for the hundredth time that his pistol was loaded. "Get me out of this mess!"

Down on the floor in the study, beneath the shattered window, he listened for any hint that somebody was approaching the house. He had no idea how many men might be out there in the darkness, only that there must be at least one, and he felt fairly sure that the first shot had only missed him by a few inches. Shattered glass lay all around him on the floor, and Thomas felt his mind racing as he tried to work out exactly what to do next.

Next to him, the boxes filled with explosive material sat in the fire's flickering light.

"George?" Thomas called out tentatively, still hoping against hope that his associate might return with a plan to fix everything. After all, George had always been in charge. "I don't mean to pressure you," he continued, "but if you happen to be here, now would be a good moment to let me know."

He waited, and he could feel his heart racing with such force that it seemed poised to burst out of his chest, yet he realized now that George had been gone for at least a day. How, he wondered, had he not been more worried? Had that infernal Mrs. Baxter managed to distract him so completely with her offers of food?

Looking down at his damaged arm, he saw scratches on the exposed bone, and he felt a knot of nausea in his belly as he realized that he had eaten the meat himself.

"This is not right," he whimpered. "There is no -"

Suddenly he heard a girl's cry. Looking at the open door that led into the hallway, he only now remembered the little girl who had suddenly appeared in the house. He heard the sound of scrabbling, scrambling footsteps racing across the wooden boards, followed by the thud of a door. A few seconds later he heard a second, much calmer set of footsteps.

"Who's there?" he called out as fresh tears ran down his face. "Please..."

Fanny Baxter's ghostly figure stepped into the doorway, staring through at him.

"What vile evil is this?" Thomas simpered, and now he couldn't understand how or why he had ever trusted this awful woman. "Who are you truly?" he shouted angrily. "*What* are you?"

"I," she replied firmly, "am the housekeeper of this place. And you, I am afraid to say, are an intruder."

"But what are you?" he asked. "Please, just tell me."

"I have already told you," she continued. "I am the housekeeper. It is my job to look after Hadlow House and its legitimate occupiers. At the moment, for reasons beyond my control, there is no master living here, so I must simply make the house habitable and ensure that I am ready whenever a new master arrives. One of the most important elements of that task, as it turns out, is the extermination of any vermin that might enter the property. And in case there is any misunderstanding here, Mr. Vowles, you should be under no illusion about the fact that you are vermin."

"Will you help me?" he sobbed.

"No, I will not," she replied. "I said just now that there is no master here at Hadlow House, and that is true, but the previous master was cruelly betrayed by his own family. While I wait for somebody else to occupy the house, I feel that I must go to certain lengths in order to avenge my master's legacy."

She turned and looked at the door for a moment, before reaching out with her right hand and digging her fingernails into the wood. Slowly, and with great care, she used those nails to start carving lines into the door itself, until she had completed the initials H.H. and stepped back.

"Hadlow House," she explained, "has such potential to be a grand, important property, and I believe that it will get there one day. Until then, I can only do my very best. But for now, you will have to excuse me, for there is a certain young girl hiding somewhere here and I really need to find her."

With that, Fanny turned and stepped out of view.

"Wait!" Thomas hissed, leaning forward before stopping as he realized that he could hear footsteps coming from somewhere outside. "Mrs. Baxter, come back!" he continued. "I have need of you! Can we not, perhaps, come to some form of agreement?"

He listened for a response, but there was now no sign of her at all. A moment later, hearing more footsteps, he looked up just in time to see a silhouetted figure appear at the broken window. Realizing that he was mostly hidden from sight behind the boxes filled with explosives, he watched as a man peered into the house, and then – very slowly – Thomas raised his pistol and aimed it at the figure. He waited for a few seconds while trying to check the tremor in his hand, and then he told himself that George would want him to take action.

Pulling the trigger to fire the pistol, he immediately heard a cry of pain from outside as the figure slumped out of sight, and he realized that for the first time in his life he had shot a man.

Perhaps, even, he had *killed* a man.

Feeling a renewed sense of determination, he told himself that he might actually be able to fight his way out of the house and escape. He still had no idea what had happened to George, but he supposed that his associate would be able to take care of himself, and that doubtless they would meet up again and resume their plan. For now, Thomas reasoned that he simply had to get himself out of danger, and that he would succeed for one very simple reason.

He knew, deep down, that he had God on his side.

CHAPTER TWENTY-SIX

"TELL HANNAH..."

As those words left Joshua Marden's lips, his body twitched and his head fell back. The shot from inside the house had blown apart the upper left side of his shoulder, and although he'd been dragged away by the other men they'd all realized immediately that he couldn't be saved. His eyes almost blinked now as he looked up at the night sky, and then he let out one final low sigh before falling still.

Reaching over, Daniel gently closed the dead man's eyes.

"Now what?" Adam Turner asked, before turning and looking back over at Hadlow House. "Can we storm in there and kill the bastard yet?"

"We don't know how much ammunition he

might have," Daniel pointed out.

"He's killed one of us!" Adam snapped angrily. "Are we just supposed to sit here and take that?"

"No, of course not," Daniel replied, watching the house carefully, "but I don't want to go barreling in there either. This Vowles fellow obviously has a good aim, and cornered men are often the most dangerous of all. I'm already going to have to go and tell Hannah Marden that her husband is dead. I'd rather not be forced to pay similar calls to any other wives in Cobblefield tonight."

"Then what do we do?" Jethro Mann asked. "Wait it out? Let the fellow starve?"

"Perhaps we are not the right people for this fight," John Constable suggested. "I mean that not in a cowardly manner, simply that this Vowles fellow seems very well prepared for such a battle. Is there not some way we can keep him contained while we wait for reinforcements?"

"We need to be clever about this," Daniel said, "and show the whole country that the people of Cobblefield are willing to make a stand for our king."

"Our barely English king," Jethro murmured. "He is still from the line of Hanover."

"That is of no concern to us," Daniel replied angrily. "Any man who -"

Before he could finish, they all heard

another cry of terror ringing out from the house. This time the sound was a little clearer, and Daniel immediately took a step toward the edge of the garden as he reached for his pistol.

"That was no woman," Morton Thatch observed. "It sounded more like -"

"A young girl," Daniel replied, lost in thought as he felt a growing sense of fear starting to rise up through his body. "It even sounded like..."

He hesitated, before shaking his head.

"No, it can't be," he continued, trying to convince himself. "She's safe at home in bed and -"

"Help me!" Anne screamed somewhere far off inside the house, and now there could be no mistake. "Please!"

"That's my granddaughter," Daniel said firmly, turning to the other men. "I don't know what she's doing out here, but I have to get her out of that house. I was urging caution before, I grant you that, but now there can be no doubt what we must do. I'm going to storm the place and I'll be glad of any man who joins me, but I shan't badmouth any of you who prefer to hold back."

"We're all with you," John Constable told him, as he raised his pistol. "I think I speak for all the men when I say that it's time we take this bastard down."

***

Too scared to even breathe, Anne pulled back into the darkness of the small cupboard into which she'd just crawled. Having scurried around trying to find somewhere to hide, and having occasionally spotted a glimpse of the terrifying woman, she had now taken refuge in one of the low cupboards in the kitchen's far corner. There was barely enough space for her to squeeze into, but she'd just about managed to pull the door shut and now she was praying that she hadn't been spotted.

A moment later she heard the slow, low creaking sound of a nearby door being pushed open.

"Please," Anne said silently, hoping that somehow she might be heard by some higher power, "get me out of here."

She was shaking with fear now, and although she tried to stop herself she quickly found that she could not; she knew she risked drawing attention to her hiding place, yet somehow she was unable to get her body fully under control. She tried to pull back even deeper into the darkness, hoping against hope that she might even be able to disappear entirely, but at the same time she felt sure she could hear slow footsteps approaching the other side of the cupboard's door.

"My child," she heard a cold, dead voice saying finally, "why do you run from me like this? Don't you know that it's futile?"

Reaching up, Anne clamped a trembling hand over her own mouth, trying to make sure that she couldn't let out another inadvertent scream.

"You have been placed in this situation by the choices of others," the voice continued, seemingly a little closer now. "I appreciate that fact, but it is not my fault. The truth is, members of your family have shown extreme disloyalty since they first set foot in this hallowed house. They could have been so happy if they had just learned what was best for them, but instead they refused to listen. What must happen tonight is merely the natural consequence of their foolishness."

Anne heard one final footstep, and this was indisputably just beyond the cupboard's door.

"Will *you* at least do the right thing?" the voice asked. "Come out so that you can meet the fate your grandmother's actions have created for you."

Anne realized after a moment that even her teeth were chattering with fear now.

"Or do you share that foul woman's cowardice?" the voice added. "Very well, then. This really doesn't have very much to do with you, anyway. It's all about teaching that wretched Patience a lesson that she will never forget."

A moment later the cupboard's door began to shift slightly, and Anne instinctively reached out to try to hold it shut. She could feel a force on the other side, pulling with growing strength, and now the little girl made no effort to hide her presence as instead she pulled on the door with all her power and tried to keep it shut.

Suddenly a gunshot rang out in the distance, followed by several more. Men's voices erupted into a fit of shouting, and there was the sound of wood splitting followed by more shouts and a thunder of footsteps.

"Help me!" Anne shouted, still just about managing to keep the door shut. "Get her away from me!"

"You really don't understand, do you?" the voice on the door's other side sneered. "I'm merely trying to put right a great wrong that was committed against this house. Against me!"

With that, the door jolted open a little more. Anne instinctively adjusted her grip, grabbing the door's edge and somehow managing to keep it from opening any further, but a moment later she saw another set of fingers reaching around from the other side, and these fingers were pale and lifeless.

"Come out of there!" the woman's voice snarled as more shots and cries rang out from elsewhere in the house. "You know it's only a matter of time. I have planned this moment perfectly, and I *will* have my revenge on your foul family!"

"Leave me alone!" Anne screamed, pulling

on the door with all her remaining strength. "I'm not going to go with you!"

"This way!" a man's voice shouted in the distance. "He's up -"

In that moment another shot thundered through the house, accompanied by a loud cry and then a series of heavy thuds as if a body had just fallen down the stairs. Anne had no idea how many men were in the house now, but she heard more shots as she tried desperately to hold the door shut. She could still see the dead woman's hand trying to pull in the opposite direction, and now the little girl was screaming constantly as she pulled as hard as she could manage. Voices were still shouting in the distance, shots were still ringing out and bodies were still falling, but all Anne knew was that she had to keep the cupboard door closed at all costs.

And then, just as she was starting to think that she might have a chance, the door was ripped open. Falling back, Anne turned away and raised her arms in one last attempt to protect herself, and then she cried out again as she felt hands reaching into the cupboard and grabbing her by the shoulders.

"Anne?"

Startled, she turned and saw a familiar face staring in at her.

"We'll talk about what you're doing here later," her grandfather, Daniel, said angrily as yet another shot fired somewhere far off in the house. "Right now, I'm getting you out of here!"

CHAPTER TWENTY-SEVEN

"THAT MAN IS WELL-ARMED," Adam Turner said as Daniel carried Anne through to the bottom of the stairs. "He has killed three of us already. Jethro is the latest."

"Take the girl," Daniel said firmly.

"Daniel -"

"Take her!" Daniel hissed, as he began to hand his sobbing granddaughter over. "Carry her out of here and take her far away, beyond the aim of any pistol."

"I will not leave the fight," Adam said firmly.

"This girl is not to be harmed," Daniel replied, before turning just as John Constable and Morton Thatch stumbled down the stairs. "She's my granddaughter and I'm ordering you to take her away from here."

"I don't want to leave you!" Anne sobbed, trying to reach over to him as Adam took her in his arms. "What if that woman comes back?"

"There is no woman here," Daniel told her firmly. "There is only one very dangerous and very treacherous fiend who will shortly be dragged out and dealt with."

"There was a woman trying to get me," Anne cried, with fresh tears rolling down her face. "I swear it's true! Grandpa, she was trying to get me! She said she wanted to hurt me!"

"The child is delirious," Daniel replied dismissively. "Adam, get her out of here and mind that you hurry. I wouldn't put it past this Vowles rat to target even a young girl."

"I'll do what you ask," Adam replied, turning and carrying Anne to the front door, "but only because of my respect for you. I would still rather be here fighting to take down that bastard upstairs."

"Grandpa, no!" Anne screamed, trying again to get away from Adam's grip. "Watch out for the woman!"

"Who is she talking about?" John Constable asked cautiously, as more cries rang out from upstairs. "Daniel, I've seen no sign of a woman here but I've heard the stories over the years."

"Those stories are childish fairy-tales,"

Daniel told him. "The girl is out of her mind with fear, she has certainly imagined any woman that she thinks she saw tonight." He turned to Morton Thatch. "If there is any man here who truly believes that there might be a ghost within these four walls, then he had better leave. I cannot use a man who is frightened of shadows."

Looking through into the kitchen, he spotted the window where – many years earlier – he had first laid eyes upon Patience. He had been peering into the house as a young man, only for her to suddenly peer back out at his from the other side; he had perhaps not realized it at the time, but he knew now that he had fallen in love with her from that very first moment, and that he still felt this love in his heart. He desperately wanted to get home and apologize for being harsh with her earlier, but he knew there would be time for that later.

"I don't like this place," John replied

"But do you think it is haunted?" Daniel asked. "Choose your answer carefully, for it matters a great deal."

"I..."

John hesitated, glancing around for a moment, before turning to him again.

"The fiend Vowles is holed up in a bedroom upstairs," he said firmly. "We've been trying to get to him for some time now, but we don't know how much ammunition he might yet have. Anyone who goes near the room is in danger."

Daniel turned and looked at the door, and he could just make out Adam carrying Anne away into the forest. In that moment he knew that his granddaughter was safe, and that the time had come for someone to make a stand and deal with Thomas Vowles once and for all.

"I want every man to wait down here," he said finally, "while I go up and speak to the miscreant. If there is even the tiniest shred of honor or dignity left in his miserable body, then he might yet be reasoned with."

"You can't go alone," Morton Thatch said. "It's too dangerous."

"On the contrary," Daniel replied, turning and looking up the stairs, "I believe this might be the only way to end this standoff without further bloodshed. I am going to try to speak with the man." He checked for a moment that his pistol was loaded. "But if that fails," he added, "then I shall not hesitate to use force."

***

Reaching the top of the stairs, Daniel looked across the landing and immediately saw that while two doors remained shut, only one of them was riddled with holes. He hesitated, listening to the silence of the house, and then he looked back down at the gathered men at the foot of the staircase.

For a few seconds, all he could think of was Patience. He remembered once again the first time he'd met her, and the first time he'd set foot in Hadlow House all those years ago. He felt his heart miss a beat as he recalled the love he'd felt for her, and the times they'd met on the little stone bridge over the river. Although he felt absolutely certain that he could handle himself, and that he'd easily be able to out-shoot Thomas Vowles if necessary, he had to admit that a flicker of fear had taken root in his chest.

Turning, he looked at the door and realized that there was no more time to waste.

"Thomas Vowles!" he called out. "You are -"

"Stay back!" Thomas could be heard gasping from the room. "I'm warning you!"

"How do you really think this is going to end?" Daniel asked. "You have killed three good men tonight, but there remain more than enough of us to take you down. After everything you've done, don't you think it's finally time to accept your fate?"

"Shut up!" Thomas snapped. "I don't even want to hear your voice!"

"If you come quietly," Daniel replied, "then I shall personally guarantee your safe passage until you can be handed over to the proper authorities. After they have taken you, I can make no promises, but I can at least assure you that you will not end up hanging from the gallows in Cobblefield like your friend."

"I want to talk to George!" Vowles gasped.

"George Jones is dead, and his body is on full public display. If you want to avoid the same fate, you must let me help you."

He waited for an answer.

"You will face death," he added, "but there are many different types of death and I can help you avoid the worst. Can you not find some honor in that, Mr. Vowles?"

He waited again, before stepping forward.

"If not -"

Suddenly the door ahead began to open. Daniel immediately raised his pistol and aimed; Thomas Vowles, appearing in the doorway, began to do the same, only to hesitate as he saw that he was already targeted.

"I never wanted any part of this!" Thomas shouted angrily, his face flushed with desperation. "I said I'd help George, but in truth I only did it for adventure! I thought it would be fun!"

"What happened to your arm?" Daniel asked, keeping the pistol trained on him. "It looks like it has been chewed by an animal."

"I want to go home," Thomas whimpered. "I just want to get on a boat and go home, and then I want to forget all about wars and fighting and all the rest."

"It's too late for that," Daniel told him.

"Why?" Thomas sobbed. "It was all George's fault, he's the one who came up with the whole plan! I was just doing what I was told!"

"That doesn't make you innocent," Daniel said with a sigh. "You will be judged by God, but there is still time for you to atone for your sins. I make no promises about your soul, but I *will* help you as much as I can!"

"Lower your gun!" Thomas sneered. "Show that you trust me!"

"I cannot do that until you have put your own weapon down," Daniel told him. "I'm sorry, but I have a wife waiting at home and I desperately want to go back to her tonight. I'm afraid that I cannot trust a man who has shown willingness to attack my king, but I have offered you a deal and I implore you to take it." He paused as he saw that Thomas was tightening his grip on his own pistol. "And I beg you," he added, "not to do anything rash or foolish. I do not want to kill you on this day, but if you make a move I shall have no hesitation."

"I'm not guilty of anything!" Thomas whimpered. "I've just been told what to do, that's all! George was the one who made all the plans! He's the one who gathered the explosives and arranged everything else, I was just obeying orders!"

"Will you come with me, then?" Daniel asked, still aiming at the man. "Will you end this madness right now? Are you a strong enough fellow to be -"

Before he could finish, he heard the unmistakable sound of a door creaking open to his left. He knew he couldn't afford to take his eyes off Thomas Vowles for a second, but he quickly realized that he was being watched. Glancing to his left, he saw a figure standing in the darkness of one of the other bedrooms, and as his eyes adjusted he realized that – even thought he hadn't seen her in more than fifty years – he recognized this woman.

Staring back at him, seeing the shock in his eyes, Fanny Baxter allowed herself a thin, slow smile.

Suddenly Daniel heard a clicking sound. Shaken from his stupor, he turned back to Thomas Vowles, but in that instant he was a fraction of a second too late. Thomas, having raised his gun, let out an angry cry and pulled the trigger.

CHAPTER TWENTY-EIGHT

"I DON'T KNOW THAT this will be the end of you," Patience said, standing in the grave with the shovel raised high above her head, ready to bring it smashing down onto the bones of Fanny Baxter, "but I can only believe that it is a start, and that it is the right thing to do."

She adjusted her grip for a moment as she prepared to summon the necessary strength.

"Rot in Hell, Fanny," she sneered. "That's where you belong."

With that, she brought the shovel crashing down, slamming the metal tip into Fanny's skull. The bone immediately shattered and crumpled, but for Patience this wasn't enough so she raised the shovel and then struck again, smashing the other side of the skull. Taking a step back, she then directed her fury at the ribs, breaking several of them instantly as she felt a rush of anger running through her body.

"This is for my mother," she added, smashing the other side of the ribs.

She took a moment to get her breath back.

"This is for my father," she said, crushing the ribs again.

She raised the shovel.

"This is for poor Father Ward!"

This time she broke one of the skeleton's arms, before holding the shovel up again.

"And this is for any other poor souls you killed," she added. "I don't believe for one second that there aren't other victims who -"

Suddenly a laugh rang out, filling the night air. Startled, Patience turned and looked around, but the laugh seemed to be somehow hanging in the air and a moment later she looked down and saw that the partially-smashed skull appeared to be twitching as it rested in the dirt, while the nearby jawbone was jumping slightly, almost as if even in their broken state the bones were causing the laughter.

"Why do you laugh?" Patience asked as she felt a growing sense of fear in her chest. "What could possibly be amusing about this? You are about to be consigned to the depths of Hell, so why -"

And then it hit her, a powerful wave of grief

and sorrow that slammed into her body and knocked her back against the grave's wall. She dropped the shovel, and in that moment she was filled with the absolute certainty that something or someone was lost. No matter how hard she tried to rid herself of this sensation, no matter how she tried to convince herself that she was overreacting, she still felt as if her heart itself had been ripped out of her chest and torn into pieces, and after a few more seconds this fear began to coalesce and take a clearer form in her mind.

"Daniel," she whispered.

She shook her head, convinced that she had to be wrong and that Daniel – wherever he might be at that moment – was absolutely fine. Nevertheless, the fear was growing in her chest until she realized that her hands were starting to shake, and now she found herself thinking of Hadlow House waiting out there in the darkness. As the cackling laughter continued all around, she was struck by the certain sense that Daniel had ended up at that house and that now something dreadful had happened.

"No," she stammered as tears filled her eyes, "it's not possible. He would never go there. Not Daniel."

The laughter grew louder still, seemingly filled her ears, and finally she looked back down at the skeletal remains of Fanny Baxter. Realizing that it was her voice that was ringing out, she grabbed the shovel and stepped forward, and then she began to rain blow after blow onto the bones, smashing them to dust with such force that she even began to break through the bottom of the coffin itself.

"It's not true!" she screamed, even as the laughter continued. "You're lying! He's fine! This is just your last attempt to drive me out of my mind but I shall never let you succeed!"

***

Stumbling on tired legs that felt as if they were about to buckle at any moment, Patience hurried along the dark road that wound through the forest. She knew she should have stayed in the village, but after leaving the cemetery – and the mocking laughter – behind she had felt as if she had no choice.

She had to prove to herself that Daniel was alive.

As soon as she saw the house ahead, she stopped in her tracks. Her mind returned to the last time she had been anywhere near the place, to that awful night when she'd just about managed to escape by climbing to freedom through the chimney. Having always sworn to never return, she felt a sense of fear hardening in her heart as – a moment later – she spotted several figures moving away from the house in the darkness, hurrying across the lawn.

"Daniel?" she gasped, racing to the gate and slipping through, then rushing across the garden in an effort to catch up to the men. "Daniel!" she called out. "Daniel, where are you?"

"Patience, stop!" Morton Thatch said, hurrying to meet her and putting his hands on the sides of her arms, trying to hold her back. "Patience, you mustn't go any further!"

"Why not?" she shouted. "I want to see my husband!"

"Patience," Morton said again, holding her more firmly this time, "you can't. You just... can't."

She opened her mouth to ask him again why not, but at that moment she saw that some of the dark figures nearby were setting a body on the ground. She told herself that this couldn't possibly be Daniel, that Daniel would always look after himself, but after a few seconds she pushed past Morton and hurried once again across the grass.

"Patience, wait!" Morton called after her. "You shouldn't see this!"

"Where is he?" she asked, slipping around some of the other men and then dropping to the ground. "Daniel, are you alright? Daniel, say something!"

In the moonlight, she could make out Daniel's familiar shirt and tunic, and the silver ring that he always wore on one finger. When she looked at his face, however, she was unable to see his features, and she found herself struggling to understand exactly what was wrong. Reaching up, she tried to remove the hat or whatever other item must be obscuring his face, but instead her fingertips simply found some kind of warm, wet meat. She fumbled some more, convinced that at any moment everything would turn out to be fine, and as she continued to search she was barely even aware of any other sounds coming from nearby.

"No," she whispered, "Daniel, you have to be fine. You just have to be."

"You were offered a chance," John Constable was saying nearby, as he and a couple of other men held Thomas Vowles firmly. "We all heard Daniel Purkiss offering to guarantee your safe passage, but you did this to him instead!"

"Please," Thomas cried, "have some mercy, I was only defending myself from -"

Before he could finish, John punched him hard in the face, before pulling him down and then kicking him so hard that he immediately broke several ribs. Barely able to breathe now, Thomas dropped to his knees and gasped for air, but he gained only a fraction of a second's respite before his head was tilted back and John punched him again, this time breaking his jaw.

"Shouldn't we question him?" one of the other men asked.

"What's the point?" John replied, staring with disgust at Thomas as blood ran freely from his lips. "Most likely he and George Jones were working alone, and now their little plot is all in ruins. All that's left to do is punish this bastard for what he's done."

"Please," Thomas groaned, as one of his teeth slipped out, "I only -"

"Silence!" John snapped, punching him again, this time splitting the skin around one eye. "Nobody here wants to hear any more of your foul excuses! You had your chance and now it's time for you to face your fate!"

As the beating continued, Patience moved around to the other side of Daniel's body. She was still trying to make sense of the mess she saw, but after a moment she was just about able to make out one dead eye staring up from the meaty mulch of his face. She also saw a row of teeth sticking out at a crooked angle, as if his entire face had been blasted away, but she still couldn't quite bring herself to accept this awful truth. Even as she ran her blood-stained hands against what was left of her husband's features, she clung to the hope that somehow she might yet be able to bring him back.

And as she finally leaned down and clutched his body, hugging him tight and sobbing wildly, she tried to ignore not only the sound of Thomas Vowles suffering nearby, but also the sound of

Fanny Baxter's laughter echoing out from somewhere deep inside Hadlow House.

CHAPTER TWENTY-NINE

"THOMAS VOWLES," JOHN CONSTABLE said the following morning, standing on the grass verge opposite *The Shoemaker* in Cobblefield, "do you have anything to say before you face your final judgment?"

Standing next to the post, with a rope tied tight around his neck, Thomas Vowles was barely even recognizable. Having been beaten all through the night, his face was bloodied and swollen, with thick splits having opened up around his mouth and cheeks. One eye was entirely swollen shut, while the other was just about able to remain open despite its broken socket. Staring straight ahead, Thomas hesitated for a moment before looking up to see George's body hanging from the top of the post.

"If you have nothing to say," John continued

through gritted teeth, as he took hold of the rope's other end, "then -"

"I was not the architect of any of this," Thomas stammered suddenly, barely able to get any words out at all since his lips were swollen and cracked and most of his teeth were gone. Even now, fresh blood leaked out and ran over the older, drier blood that was caked around the corners of his mouth. "I am, indeed, the greatest victim. I merely followed a man I believed to be good, for a cause that seemed right to me."

He stared up at George for a moment longer and saw that a dark bird was perched on the dead man's shoulder. After a few seconds he realized that the bird was picking at the flesh on George's face, and he understood that he too would soon suffer such a fate.

Suddenly a rock slammed into George's body, and Thomas turned to see two young boys at the edge of the crowd. The boys each had several rocks in their hands, and they began to throw them up at the corpse while excitedly discussing how many points they had scored against one another in some kind of macabre game.

"We have failed, that much is certain," Thomas continued, turning to the others, "but I do not see that this means our cause was wrong, or that it is lost." He took as deep a breath as he could manage. "I maintain that the colonies -"

"Enough of this heresy!" John spat, before pulling on the rope. A few other men began to help. "Let us silence this man forever!"

As the rope tightened still further around his neck and began to lift him up, Thomas was unable to keep himself from struggling. He had hoped to remain resilient in his final moments, to show no sign of fear, but as he was hauled up to join George at the top of the post he could not hold back; spluttering and spraying blood from his mouth, he kicked wildly in thin air and began to twist. He hoped now that by some mercy his neck might snap and that his end would arrive quickly, but no such mercy came his way and he was soon alongside George, whose dead features he now saw closely for the first time.

The bird hopped over onto his shoulder and began to pick the fresher meat from around his face, and as he felt the sharp beak pecking at his features Thomas could only let out another gurgled cry of agony. At that moment, he also felt the first rock hitting him from below as the children laughed.

***

"Is he dead?" John Constable asked, sitting at a table inside the inn and staring at his mug of ale.

"I think so," Morton Thatch replied, peering out the window and watching the two bodies hanging from the post. He could see three birds now feasting on the mess, but a moment later the body on the left twitched slightly and managed another brief kick. "Ah, no," he added, "I believe there is still some life left in Mr. Vowles."

"He's been up there for almost an hour," Robertson Smothers pointed out from his seat by the bar. "That's rather impressive."

"There's nothing impressive about those two traitors," John pointed out darkly. "I don't want to hear anyone using those words about men who would conspire against our king. He deserves a slow death, though, and I'm glad to hear that's what he's getting."

Morton watched as the two boys threw some more rocks at the dying man, and then he turned and made his way over to the table.

"Has anybody spoken to Patience Purkiss?" he asked as he took a seat.

"I tried," John replied, "but this morning she is insensible. She merely sits and rocks back and forth."

"My wife and I are to take over Daniel's duties for now," Morton explained, "until some other arrangement can be made. In truth, I do not know that Patience will ever recover from what happened last night. She wouldn't even let go of her husband's corpse until we got it back to the village and morning light finally arrived."

"Women are not meant to witness such horrors," John told him. "Their minds break easily."

"Then there is the child," Morton pointed out. "Margaret and I can of course care for her, but I find myself wondering what will become of her as she grows up." He paused for a moment. "Then, of course," he added, "there is the question of the house."

"What of it?" Robertson Smothers asked.

"What is to be done about it?" Morton replied. "It is still owned by Patience Purkiss and her family, but I daresay that they will have no further use for it now. Until recently it was occupied by her father Samuel but now it stands empty. I do not believe that it can remain that way forever."

"And *I* do not believe that it is any of our business," John told him.

"But -"

"It is far enough out from the village that nobody needs to go near it," John continued, "or even see it. We have all long known that there is something evil about that place, and that fear has only been confirmed now."

"We believe that Patience dug up the body of the old housekeeper last night," Robertson reminded the others. "She left a real mess in one of the graves, the bones were all wrecked and had turned to little more than dust."

"We'll have the body reburied," John told

him, "and that will be the end of the matter. In truth, few need to know what happened there."

"But the house itself," Morton replied, "can't be left to -"

"Do what you want about the house!" John snapped angrily, getting to his feet and turning to him. "Do you think anybody cares? It belongs to the Purkiss family now, but knock it down if that is what you wish! Burn it! Turn it to ash and then salt the ground!"

"I would need Patience's permission."

"Then get it!" John hissed. "If you can, at least. After everything that has happened, I do not care one iota about some jumbled pile of bricks out there in the forest, but if Hadlow House disturbs you so much then by all means take matters into your own hands! I doubt that there is a man here who will stop you!"

"I cannot act without speaking to Patience first," Morton replied. "I believe she must be consulted."

"Then consult her," John said, grabbing his mug and finishing the last of his ale before heading toward the front door. "I don't know about the rest of you," he continued, "but I would like very much to never think or hear of Hadlow House ever again. Do what you want, but for the love of all that's holy let us not speak of the place. And now, if you'll excuse me, I am going to focus on more practical matters, such as arranging for Daniel Purkiss to rest properly in the cemetery. Any other talk, about houses or evil or such matters, are of no interest to me whatsoever."

Once John had left, the others sat in silence for a few minutes. Nobody knew quite what to say, until finally Morton got to his feet and finished his ale.

"I must go to Patience," he said with a sigh.

"Are you sure that's wise?" William Barton asked from the far corner. "Do you think you'll even get a proper answer from her?"

"I think I must try," Morton replied, turning and heading toward the door. "Despite everything that has happened, there must still be some sense in her mind somewhere."

As soon as he was outside, Morton stopped to watch as the children threw more stones at Thomas Vowles. He watched the body hanging from the post, and after a couple of minutes he realized that the man was finally dead. Turning, he began to walk around the corner, heading toward the yard while – high above him – a crow pulled out the eyeball from the face of the dead man and then flew away with its prize.

CHAPTER THIRTY

SITTING ALONE IN THE kitchen, Anne stared at the chessboard for a moment longer before moving one of the pieces. She considered this move for a few more seconds, before stepping around the table and sitting on the other side, where she began to contemplate her reply.

"Are you still playing that game?" Margaret Thatch asked as she made her way through, carrying some old metal bowls. "How can you play if you have no opponent?"

"I'm just practicing for when Grandma's feeling better again."

"Sweetheart," Margaret replied, "I wouldn't count on that happening too soon."

"Why not?"

"Your grandmother is feeling a little...

tired," she explained cautiously. "She went through a lot last night. Indeed, she has been through a lot over the past few years and I think she needs to rest and think about it all. That happens to adults sometimes, they have to take time to work things out in their minds. And that is especially true of women, because we tend to find these things harder than men."

"Can I go up and see her?"

"Not right now."

"But when?"

"When she's feeling a little better."

"When might that be?"

"A while," Margaret said, struggling to think of ways to answer the girl's questions without revealing too much. "I don't know how to play that game, but if you were to show me, I might try to match you."

"It's alright," Anne replied, "I'd rather wait until Grandma's ready. And if I practice really hard, then I might be much better than her by the time she comes back downstairs."

"Do you think I'm too stupid to understand the rules?"

"I don't know," Anne said with a shrug, while still examining the pieces. "It's a game for Grandma and me, that's all. If you don't mind, I'd rather wait for her."

"Of course," Margaret said, smiling even as

tears reached her eyes. "It's always better to hope for the best than to surrender and assume that..."

Her voice trailed off as she found herself once again lost for words. A moment later she was hugely relieved to hear footsteps entering the hallway, and she turned just in time to see her husband Morton making his way through.

"There you are!" she said, still somehow managing to maintain her smile. "I was just telling young Anne that I would like to learn that game she's playing."

"A fine idea," Morton replied, stopping next to her and leaning close to her ear. "I must go upstairs and speak to Patience for a moment."

"Is that wise?" Margaret whispered.

"I do not know, but she cannot be ignored. Several hours have passed now and I can only hope that she has perhaps regained some of her senses." He glanced at Anne, who was now busy moving the chess pieces again. After a moment, he pulled a silver ring from his pocket and held it up so that his wife could see the initials D.P. on the side. "I retrieved this from Daniel's body before it was taken to be prepared. I thought that Patience might like it. It's a small thing, but you never know what might help."

"Perhaps you're right," she replied, "and it is certainly worth a try." She glanced over at Anne again and saw that the girl was absorbed in her game. "The sooner Patience is up and about, the sooner young Anne might feel more comforted. I'm not sure whether she truly understands that her grandfather is dead, but if she doesn't, Patience would be the best person to break the news."

"I'll do my best to get through to her," Morton told her. "I might be some time up there, however. Wish me luck."

***

Having knocked at the door to the bedroom, Morton took a moment to wait for any response. He felt a growing sense of unease in his chest, but he told himself that his worst fears were unlikely to come true. For as long as he had known Patience, he had understood her to be a strong and stable woman. Surely, he reasoned now, she was bound to pull through and take Daniel's death in her stride.

After a few seconds, he knocked again.

"Patience?" he said cautiously, wondering whether she might be sleeping. "I really do not wish to trouble you, but there are a few matters that must be dealt with swiftly. Would you mind if I come in?"

Again he waited, and then he turned the door's handle and pushed it open. He expected to see a resting shape on the bed, but to his surprise he saw instead that the curtain were drawn and the bed was empty.

"Patience? Are you decent?"

Stepping into the darkened room, he noticed a slightly fusty smell in the air. He stopped and looked around, but he was starting to wonder whether Patience might somehow have slipped out of the house without being seen, in which case he really wasn't sure where she might have gone. He thought of her wandering off into the countryside, or perhaps seeking safety and refuge back at that awful house in the forest.

"Damn it," he muttered, turning to go back and find his wife, "what shall I do about -"

Stopping suddenly, he realized that he could see a figure sitting on the floor in the far corner, barely visible in the shadows. He hesitated, wondering whether he might in fact be mistaken, and then as he took one more step forward he realized that this was indeed Patience Purkiss, and that he could just about hear her muttering away to herself under her breath.

"Patience?" he said cautiously. "How are you feeling? Would you like me to fetch Margaret?"

He was on the verge of doing just that, yet something compelled him to stay. After a moment he held up the silver ring, hoping that it might jog her memory. The ring was just a small thing, a silly trinket perhaps, yet he had never known Daniel without it, and he wanted desperately to show poor

Patience a little mark of kindness.

"I brought this for you," he continued. "It belonged to Daniel, as I'm sure you recall. I don't know, perhaps it's a foolish thing, but I suppose I hoped that some small reminder of him might help." He waited for a response, before placing the ring on the table next to the bed. "I'll leave it here," he added. "Patience, I have been talking to some of the other men about Hadlow House, about what should be done with the place. I know you might not be ready to talk about it, but I was thinking that a few of us might go out there this afternoon and just take a look around. We don't know exactly what Vowles and Jones left there, but there was talk of perhaps some explosives and other items that should be retrieved and made safe."

Again he waited, but he was starting to think that fetching his wife really might be the best option after all. Women, he had found over the years, could be terribly confusing creatures but the one saving grace was that they seemed able to understand one another.

"Wait here," he said, turning to once again leave the room, "I shall bring Margaret up and -"

"Don't go there!" Patience hissed, her voice sounding impossibly dark and scratchy as it loomed from the shadows.

He stopped and looked back at her.

"Don't go to that house!" she added. "Do

you hear me?"

"We only mean to go for an hour or two," he explained. "To make it safe, as I told you."

"You will not go anywhere near that place," she replied. "No-one will. The house belongs to me, and as long as I am alive no-one will ever even set eyes on it again. Do you understand me?"

"Patience -"

"She's still there!" she snarled. "She'll always be there, always waiting and plotting! I think I harmed her, I think by destroying her earthly remains I stopped her reaching out any further, but nothing can ever remove her from that place entirely! I will not stand for anyone ever going near Hadlow House ever again!"

"I understand," he told her, still trying to think of a better way to get his point across. "However, Patience, I *do* feel that it would be a good idea to have someone take a look around the place. A few of us shall go up and see that all is fit to be left, and make sure that everything is as it should be and... put it all in order. The house cannot simply be abandoned as -"

"Why aren't you listening to me?" she asked angrily, stirring a little in the shadows, leaning forward but still not quite emerging from the darkness. "No-one is to go up there. Why is that so hard for you to understand? I want Fanny Baxter's ghost to rot alone for the rest of eternity with no hope of ever claiming another soul! I won't let anyone else fall into another of her traps!"

"Patience, no-one is talking about ghosts," he replied. "I just think -"

"No!" she screamed, suddenly scrambling to her feet and lunging at him. Wild-eyed and frantic, her features filled with madness, she grabbed Morton and slammed him against the wall. "Never! Do you hear me?" she shouted at the top of her voice, as if her mind had broken forever. "No-one else will ever again go anywhere near Hadlow House!"

EPILOGUE

OUT IN THE FOREST, beneath a gray afternoon sky, dead trees lay upon the ground. Nobody had been out to this part of the forest for quite some time, since the poaching away from the river was not so lucrative. Besides, of late, even the animals of the forest had stayed away from this area.

A moment later the silence was broken by shuffling footsteps. Oliver Baxter lumbered into view, stumbling slightly as his one good arm swung from his side. He stopped, looking ahead and spotting the first faint hint of Hadlow House's roof beyond the line of trees. He furrowed his brow for a moment, as if trying to remember something that remained just out of reach, and then he turned and walked away, heading off in a different direction in search of some lost possession that drew him ever onward.

Closer to the house, a man stood near the window, seemingly lost in his own silent confusion. The ghostly figured of Joshua Marsden was covered in his own blood, but he seemed barely aware of the massive injury to his shoulder. Instead he simply stared for a few seconds at the spot where he'd died, before turning away and fading out of sight. Now the garden was empty, the only movement coming from the faint breeze that blew the branches of the old oak tree.

Inside Hadlow House, silence reigned. In the dining room, a figure sat all alone in the gloom; her hands were resting on the table and her gaze was focused on the opposite wall. Had anyone leaned close to this figure, they might just have made out the very faintest of noises coming from the back of her head, where her skull had long ago been broken. Thick, fat glistening maggots were crawling through her brain, feasting on what was left of the mind of Rebecca Hadlow. On the front of her face, meanwhile, her pupils were large and her mouth hung open as if she might at any moment finally manage to let out a guttural groan.

Upstairs, an occasional creaking sound could be heard, as if a taut rope was hanging from one of the heavy wooden beams above the staircase. No such rope could be seen at that moment, yet the sound persisted and – from time to time – seemed to become a little louder, almost as if some invisible body was hanging down in the dead space.

Meanwhile, in the master bedroom, a lone figure sat on the bed. Fanny Baxter was staring at the wall opposite, where a hole remained in the brickwork above the fireplace. Many years earlier, Fanny had reached through that hole and felt a wriggling living ankle on the other side; she had tried to hold onto that ankle, only for it to slip through her grasp at the last second, but she knew deep down that she would get another chance. Her plan to claim the life of Daniel Purkiss had worked perfectly, she had moved all the pieces into place and they had obeyed her without even realizing that they were being manipulated. Now she felt renewed by Patience's cries of pain, but she knew that soon she would need more.

Always more.

Hearing a bumping sound out on the landing, she turned and saw a figure walking past the door. The ghost of Daniel Purkiss stopped and looked in at her, staring for a moment but then turning away and disappearing from view.

Fanny, meanwhile, looked back over at the hole in the wall. She might have lost her grip on that ankle more than fifty years ago, but she knew that Patience was still out there and that one day she would be lured back to Hadlow House. And until that day arrived, Fanny was simply going to expand her power and grow her strength, while coming up with some fresh way to torture Patience and bring her back under control. For Fanny was the housekeeper, and she had no intention of letting the property or its estate fall out of her reach. She simply wished to wait, biding her time until a new master might arrive.

As she continued to stare at the hole in the wall, a smile began to creep slowly across her face.

NEXT IN THIS SERIES

1800

(THE HAUNTING OF HADLOW HOUSE BOOK 4)

Everyone in Cobblefield now knows to stay away from Hadlow House. Since the horrifying events that rocked the village a quarter of a century earlier, nobody has even dared to go near the place.

One day two young girls go missing, and whispered voices suggest that they might have been last seen heading out to Hadlow House for an adventure. And one of those girls should know better, because she just so happens to be the great-granddaughter of one of the house's earliest victims.

1800 is the fourth book in the *Haunting of Hadlow House* series, which tells the story of one haunted house over the centuries from its construction to the present day. All the lives, all the souls, all the tragedies... and all the ghosts. Readers are advised to start with the first book in the series.

Also by Amy Cross

The Haunting of Nelson Street
(The Ghosts of Crowford book 1)

Crowford, a sleepy coastal town in the south of England, might seem like an oasis of calm and tranquility. Beneath the surface, however, dark secrets are waiting to claim fresh victims, and ghostly figures plot revenge.

Having finally decided to leave the hustle of London, Daisy and Richard Johnson buy two houses on Nelson Street, a picturesque street in the center of Crowford. One house is perfect and ready to move into, while the other is a fire-ravaged wreck that needs a lot of work. They figure they have plenty of time to work on the damaged house while Daisy recovers from a traumatic event.

Soon, they discover that the two houses share a common link to the past. Something awful once happened on Nelson Street, something that shook the town to its core.

Also by Amy Cross

The Revenge of the Mercy Belle
(The Ghosts of Crowford book 2)

The year is 1950, and a great tragedy has struck the town of Crowford. Three local men have been killed in a storm, after their fishing boat the Mercy Belle sank. A mysterious fourth man, however, was rescue. Nobody knows who he is, or what he was doing on the Mercy Belle... and the man has lost his memory.

Five years later, messages from the dead warn of impending doom for Crowford. The ghosts of the Mercy Belle's crew demand revenge, and the whole town is being punished. The fourth man still has no memory of his previous existence, but he's married now and living under the named Edward Smith. As Crowford's suffering continues, the locals begin to turn against him.

What really happened on the night the Mercy Belle sank? Did the fourth man cause the tragedy? And will Crowford survive if this man is not sent to meet his fate?

Also by Amy Cross

The Devil, the Witch and the Whore
(The Deal book 1)

"Leave the forest alone. Whatever's out there, just let it be. Don't make it angry."

When a horrific discovery is made at the edge of town, Sheriff James Kopperud realizes the answers he seeks might be waiting beyond in the vast forest. But everybody in the town of Deal knows that there's something out there in the forest, something that should never be disturbed. A deal was made long ago, a deal that was supposed to keep the town safe. And if he insists on investigating the murder of a local girl, James is going to have to break that deal and head out into the wilderness.

Meanwhile, James has no idea that his estranged daughter Ramsey has returned to town. Ramsey is running from something, and she thinks she can find safety in the vast tunnel system that runs beneath the forest. Before long, however, Ramsey finds herself coming face to face with creatures that hide in the shadows. One of these creatures is known as the devil, and another is known as the witch. They're both waiting for the whore to arrive, but for very different reasons. And soon Ramsey is offered a terrible deal, one that could save or destroy the entire town, and maybe even the world.

Also by Amy Cross

The Soul Auction

"I saw a woman on the beach. I watched her face a demon."

Thirty years after her mother's death, Alice Ashcroft is drawn back to the coastal English town of Curridge. Somebody in Curridge has been reviewing Alice's novels online, and in those reviews there have been tantalizing hints at a hidden truth. A truth that seems to be linked to her dead mother.

"Thirty years ago, there was a soul auction."

Once she reaches Curridge, Alice finds strange things happening all around her. Something attacks her car. A figure watches her on the beach at night. And when she tries to find the person who has been reviewing her books, she makes a horrific discovery.

What really happened to Alice's mother thirty years ago? Who was she talking to, just moments before dropping dead on the beach? What caused a huge rockfall that nearly tore a nearby cliff-face in half? And what sinister presence is lurking in the grounds of the local church?

Also by Amy Cross

Darper Danver: The Complete First Series

Five years ago, three friends went to a remote cabin in the woods and tried to contact the spirit of a long-dead soldier. They thought they could control whatever happened next. They were wrong...

Newly released from prison, Cassie Briggs returns to Fort Powell, determined to get her life back on track. Soon, however, she begins to suspect that an ancient evil still lurks in the nearby cabin. Was the mysterious Darper Danver really destroyed all those years ago, or does her spirit still linger, waiting for a chance to return?

As Cassie and her ex-boyfriend Fisher are finally forced to face the truth about what happened in the cabin, they realize that Darper isn't ready to let go of their lives just yet. Meanwhile, a vengeful woman plots revenge for her brother's murder, and a New York ghost writer arrives in town to uncover the truth. Before long, strange carvings begin to appear around town and blood starts to flow once again.

Also by Amy Cross

The Ghost of Molly Holt

"Molly Holt is dead. There's nothing to fear in this house."

When three teenagers set out to explore an abandoned house in the middle of a forest, they think they've found the location where the infamous Molly Holt video was filmed.

They've found much more than that...

Tim doesn't believe in ghosts, but he has a crush on a girl who does. That's why he ends up taking her out to the house, and it's also why he lets her take his only flashlight. But as they explore the house together, Tim and Becky start to realize that something else might be lurking in the shadows.

Something that, ten years ago, suffered unimaginable pain.

Something that won't rest until a terrible wrong has been put right.

Also by Amy Cross

American Coven

He kidnapped three women and held them in his basement. He thought they couldn't fight back. He was wrong...

Snatched from the street near her home, Holly Carter is taken to a rural house and thrown down into a stone basement. She meets two other women who have also been kidnapped, and soon Holly learns about the horrific rituals that take place in the house. Eventually, she's called upstairs to take her place in the ice bath.

As her nightmare continues, however, Holly learns about a mysterious power that exists in the basement, and which the three women might be able to harness. When they finally manage to get through the metal door, however, the women have no idea that their fight for freedom is going to stretch out for more than a decade, or that it will culminate in a final, devastating demonstration of their new-found powers.

Also by Amy Cross

The Ash House

Why would anyone ever return to a haunted house?

For Diane Mercer the answer is simple. She's dying of cancer, and she wants to know once and for all whether ghosts are real.

Heading home with her young son, Diane is determined to find out whether the stories are real. After all, everyone else claimed to see and hear strange things in the house over the years. Everyone except Diane had some kind of experience in the house, or in the little ash house in the yard.

As Diane explores the house where she grew up, however, her son is exploring the yard and the forest. And while his mother might be struggling to come to terms with her own impending death, Daniel Mercer is puzzled by fleeting appearances of a strange little girl who seems drawn to the ash house, and by strange, rasping coughs that he keeps hearing at night.

The Ash House is a horror novel about a woman who desperately wants to know what will happen to her when she dies, and about a boy who uncovers the shocking truth about a young girl's murder.

Also by Amy Cross

Haunted

Twenty years ago, the ghost of a dead little girl drove
Sheriff Michael Blaine to his death.

Now, that same ghost is coming for his daughter.

Returning to the small town where she grew up, Alex
Roberts is determined to live a normal, quiet life. For the
residents of Railham, however, she's an unwelcome
reminder of the town's darkest hour.

Twenty years ago, nine-year-old Mo Garvey was found
brutally murdered in a nearby forest. Everyone thinks
that Alex's father was responsible, but if the killer was
brought to justice, why is the ghost of Mo Garvey still
after revenge?

And how far will the real killer go to protect his secret,
when Alex starts getting closer to the truth?

Haunted is a horror novel about a woman who has to
face her past, about a town that would rather forget, and
about a little girl who refuses to let death stand in her
way.

AMY CROSS

AMY CROSS

Also by Amy Cross

The Ghosts of Hexley Airport

Ten years ago, more than two hundred people died in a
horrific plane crash at Hexley Airport.

Today, some say their ghosts still haunt the terminal
building.

When she starts her new job at the airport, working a
night shift as part of the security team, Casey assumes
the stories about the place can't be true. Even when she
has a strange encounter in a deserted part of the
departure hall, she's certain that ghosts aren't real.

Soon, however, she's forced to face the truth. Not only is
there something haunting the airport's buildings and
tarmac, but a sinister force is working behind the scenes
to replicate the circumstances of the original accident.
And as a snowstorm moves in, Hexley Airport looks set
to witness yet another disaster.

AMY CROSS

AMY CROSS

Also by Amy Cross

Asylum
(The Asylum Trilogy book 1)

"No-one ever leaves Lakehurst. The staff, the patients, the ghosts... Once you're here, you're stuck forever."

After shooting her little brother dead, Annie Radford is sent to Lakehurst psychiatric hospital for assessment. Hearing voices in her head, Annie is forced to undergo experimental new treatments devised by a mysterious old man who lives in the hospital's attic. It soon becomes clear that the hospital's staff, led by the vicious Nurse Winter, are hiding something horrific at Lakehurst.

As Annie struggles to survive the hospital, she learns more about Nurse Winter's own story. Once a promising young medical student, Kirsten Winter also heard voices in her head. Voices that traveled a long way to reach her. Voices that have a plan of their own. Voices that will stop at nothing to get what they want.

What kind of signals are being transmitted from the basement of the hospital? Who is the old man in the attic? Why are living human brains kept in jars? And what is the dark secret that lurks at the heart of the hospital?

AMY CROSS

BOOKS BY AMY CROSS

For more information, visit:

www.amycross.com

AMY CROSS

Printed in Great Britain
by Amazon

26018578R00169